Smoldering NIGHTS

USA TODAY BESTSELLING AUTHOR
PJ FIALA

I've had so many wonderful people come into my life and I want you all to know how much I appreciate it. From each and every reader who takes the time out of their days to read my stories and leave reviews, thank you.

My beautiful, smart and fun Road Queens, who play games with me, post fun memes, keep the conversation rolling and help me create these captivating characters, places, businesses and more. Thank you ladies for your ideas, support and love. The following characters and places were created by:

Angela M Carter - Sadie Anderson - Izzy's best friend

Karen Cranford LeBeau - Izzy Payton - (heroine in book 6)

Marlene Davis - Blain Davis - Mitch's employee

Terri DeMario - Mitch DeMario - (Security Specialist former Marine, Hero in book 6)

Nancy Hoch - Austin DeMario - Mitch's brother

Monique Mousseau Westwood - Iris Payton - Izzy's sister

Terra Oenning - Jayson Davis - Delilah's Assistant

Terra Oenning - Jillie - Retired lady at Petal Pushers

Shannon Lea Sidoti - Dakin De Mario - Mitch's brother

To my family, my greatest blessing and unwavering support system. Your love, encouragement, and sacrifices have made this dream possible.

And to my husband and best friend, Gene—thank you for standing beside me every step of the way. Your belief in me, your patience, and your love are the foundation of everything I do. Words will never be enough to express how much you mean to me, but I will spend my life showing you.

***

To our veterans and all those currently serving in the armed forces, police, fire departments, and as EMTs—your courage, dedication, and sacrifices do not go unnoticed. Thank you for your unwavering commitment to protecting and serving. It is with heartfelt gratitude and deep respect that I honor you here. You are the true heroes, and your contributions inspire every word on these pages.

DESCRIPTION

Grumpy Meets Sunshine. Protector Meets Independent Woman. Danger Brings Them Together.

Mitch DeMario, a former Marine and security consultant, is no stranger to danger—or heartbreak. After years on the battlefield, he's traded the chaos of combat for the quiet of Blossom Springs. But when fiery florist Izzy Payton storms into his life, she brings a new kind of challenge he's not prepared for.

Izzy Payton is a fiercely independent woman determined to protect her family's flower shop, Petal Pushers, from a string of mysterious sabotage attempts. Sabotaged deliveries and threatening notes have turned her once-peaceful life into a whirlwind of suspicion and fear. The shop, her last connection to her late father, is everything to her—and she's not about to let anyone take it away.

When Izzy hires Mitch to uncover the truth, their professional relationship quickly ignites into something neither can ignore. As danger escalates and tensions rise, Mitch's protective instincts clash with Izzy's fierce independence. Together, they'll have to navigate sabotage, secrets, and the undeniable pull of their growing connection.

Will Mitch and Izzy catch the culprit before it's too late—or will the sparks between them burn them both?

USA Today bestselling author PJ Fiala brings you a steamy, small-town romantic suspense where love blooms amidst danger. Full-length novel, no cliffhangers, and a guaranteed happily-ever-after.

Looking for stories filled with heart-pounding suspense, steamy romance, and unforgettable characters? Sign up for my newsletter and get a **FREE book** to dive into right away!

It's easy: 1 Sign up below. 2 Confirm your email (we like to keep things legit and bot-free). 3 Start enjoying your free read and exclusive updates, sneak peeks, and special offers!

Love awaits—don't miss your chance to join the adventure!

https://www.pjfiala.com/subscribe/

BLOSSOM
Springs

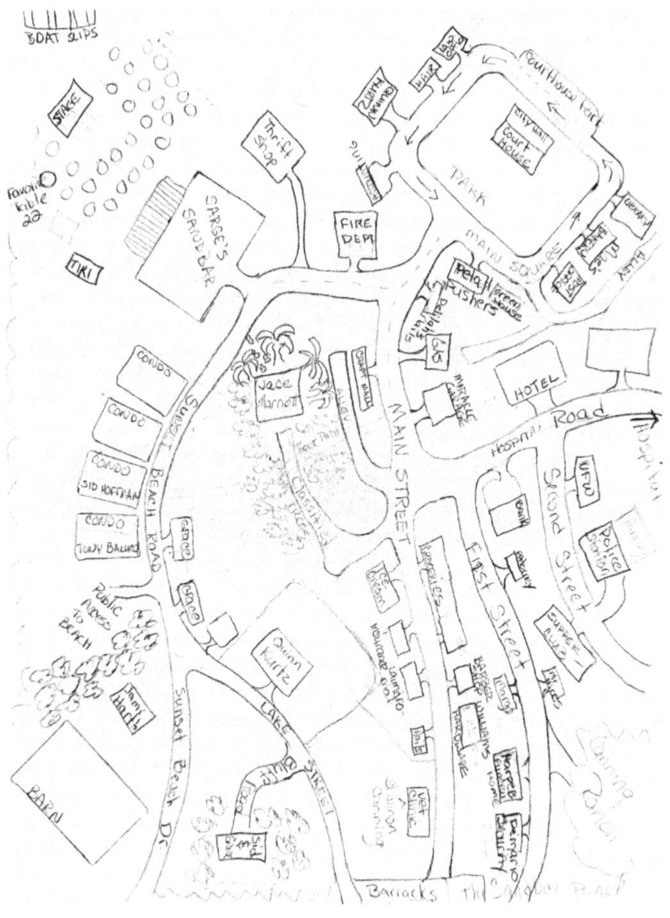

HAND DRAWN BY PJ FIALA

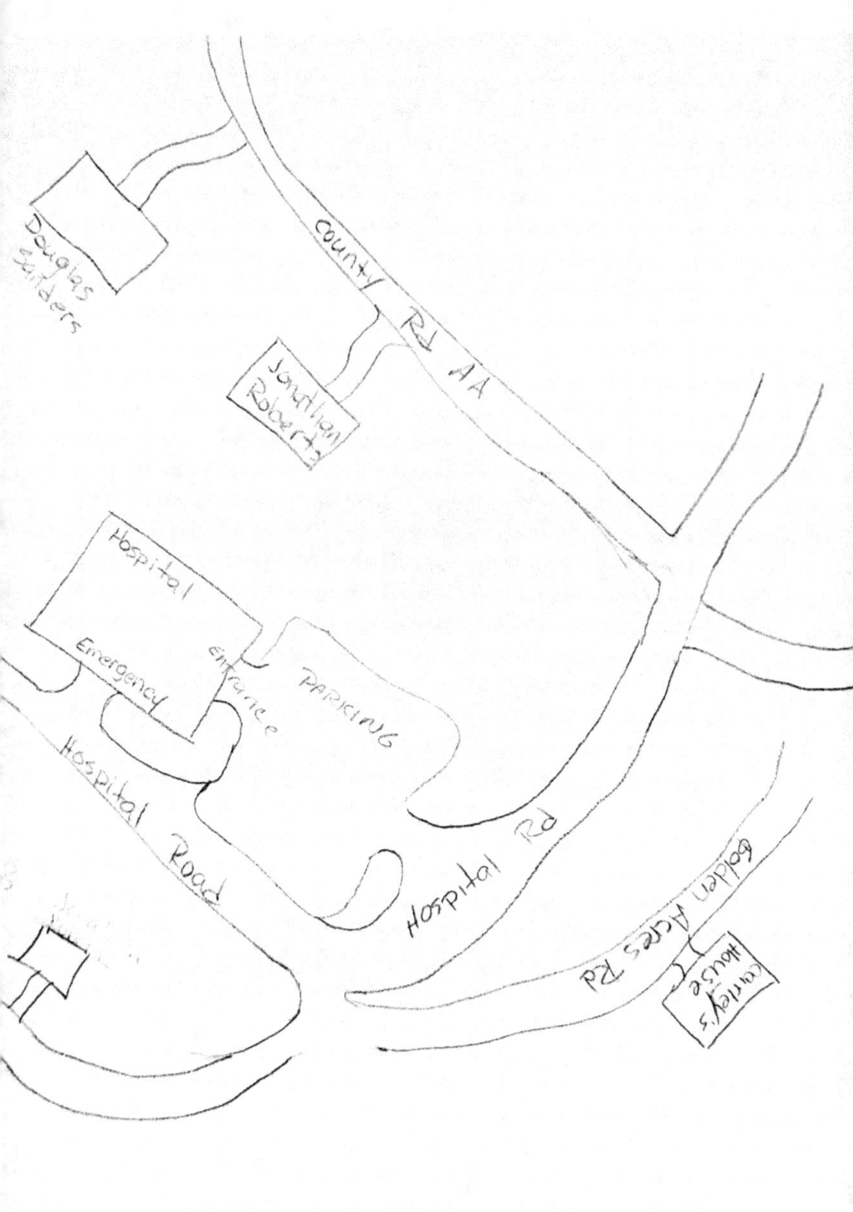

Douglas Kinders
Jonathan Roberts
County Rd AA
Hospital
Emergency
entrance
PARKING
Hospital Road
Hospital Rd
Golden Acres Rd
Carney's House

1

The antiseptic sting of hospital air hit Mitch DeMario before he even opened his eyes. The rhythmic beep of the heart monitor was steady, but every beat pulsed against the tight pressure bandage across his ribs. He gritted his teeth, shifting slightly in the hospital bed, and regretted it immediately.

Pain flared through his side like a firework. His eyes squeezed shut tightly, and that sent a roaring pulse through the back of his head.

"Take it easy," a woman said gently, adjusting the IV in his arm. "You've got a cracked rib and a mild concussion. You need to rest."

"I don't rest," Mitch muttered, pushing the bed controls to sit upright. "I recover. Fast."

He opened his eyes to a brightly lit room. It was painted a sickly tan and nondescript, with some ugly watercolor of flowers on the wall directly across from him.

The nurse who'd been administering to the monitor to his right gave him a look but didn't argue. She was middle-aged, if he had to guess, maybe mid to late forties. Near his age, if he were honest. She worked efficiently and carefully as she recorded the numbers from his monitors into the laptop on a rolling stand in front of her. Her hair was cut short, and she wore a sparkly barrette on the right side. A few silver streaks caught the sunlight as she turned her head.

She opened her mouth to speak to him, but before she could say more, the door opened, and Izzy Payton stepped in, her expression a mix of guilt, fear, and something unspoken. Her shoulders were stiff, her arms crossed tightly, and her eyes went straight to Mitch.

"You look like hell," she said softly.

He managed a weak grin. "Good to see you too."

Izzy hovered just inside the doorway, not moving closer. "I shouldn't have called you. If I hadn't..."

"Stop." Mitch's voice was firm despite the rasp. "This wasn't your fault. Someone targeted you. I walked into that willingly." Taking the breaths he needed to speak sent shards of pain through his ribs, though he tried not to show it.

Izzy's throat worked as she swallowed, nodding, but the tears shining in her eyes betrayed her composure.

"What exactly happened?" Mitch asked, cutting through the silence. "I remember pulling up. Then a noise. Heat."

"A rock sailed through the window and hit you in the chest. You fell backwards and broke one of my display shelves. You smacked the back of your head on the floor. Then, the back of the shop exploded. A propane tank we use for outdoor arrangements. It wasn't a leak, they said it was tampered with."

Mitch's jaw clenched, and he slowly inhaled. "Deliberate."

Izzy nodded. Her long blonde hair was a mess as if she'd been rolling in a hay field. It was strewn with bits of stems, a leaf stuck to the top of her head, and the ends that dropped over her slender shoulders looked as if they'd been burned.

He shifted again, trying to focus through the haze, trying to get comfortable. "Has anything else happened? Before this? Anything strange?"

She hesitated, then looked away. Poor little gal looked scared as a rabbit in a trap. "A few things. Missing deliveries. A smashed window. I thought it was bad luck. Now I'm not so sure."

Mitch met her eyes. "Someone's sending a message. And now it's loud and clear. But I've got a message of my own: they don't get to scare you. They don't get to win."

For a long second, neither of them spoke. Their eyes met and locked onto one another. The nurse who stood by listening and watching finally nodded. "I'll come back in a bit to check on you."

She silently left the room, but he and Izzy were frozen in place. He couldn't seem to make himself look away.

Then Izzy stepped forward, gripping the bed rail, her voice ragged and soft. "You shouldn't have gotten hurt."

"I've been hurt worse," Mitch said, holding her gaze. "But I won't let it happen again. I'm going to find out who's doing this. And I'm going to stop them."

"How are you going to do that? You're hurt. And I'm responsible for pulling you into this."

He lifted his right hand and laid it over hers on the bedrail. Her hand was cold, and he saw goosebumps on her arms. "You're no more responsible than that nurse who was in here. You had no idea anything like that would happen."

A tear escaped her eye and slowly tracked down her cheek. From that, he could see her face was dusty everywhere the wet tear hadn't touched. He lifted his hand slowly so as not to cause pain and pinched the leaf stuck in her hair. He grinned when he showed her what he'd pulled from her hair.

The corner of her mouth lifted slightly, "That's about the only part of a plant left in my beautiful little shop. The nursery in the back is all but decimated."

He nodded his understanding. "We'll get it fixed."

"It's a crime scene now."

"We'll get it fixed after the police are finished with it."

"I have weddings coming up and a birthday party next week, and my customers won't have flowers, and I'm going to lose my entire business, and that's how I live, plus it's all I have from my dad, and..."

"Stop. Take a breath." His chest felt heavy with the weight of her sorrow. "What's important is that you weren't hurt. Do you understand?"

Her watery eyes stared into his. After a quiet moment, she nodded her understanding.

"Good. Now, I've got some good friends and I'll bet you do too. So, you should go home and take a shower. Then lie down for a bit and rest. I'm going to work on getting myself out of here. Then, we'll meet and come up with a plan to help you fulfill orders and get your shop back up and running. I'll work on security, and we'll both work with the police to make sure your place is secure and you're protected. Understand?"

"I can't take a nap. I have to make calls. I have to see if I can remember..."

"Izzy!" He slowly took a breath. "Honey, listen to me. Go home and get some rest. I promise you'll feel better."

Another tear left a trail down her other cheek, and she daintily sniffed. He saw her lips quiver before she licked them and sucked them into her mouth.

"Are you scared?"

She nodded again, and his heart hurt for her.

2

Izzy sat as still as a cactus on a warm summer day as the doctor looked Mitch over.

"I think you can go home if you promise to wear the banding around your ribs and take it easy."

Mitch grunted. "I'll take it easy."

"And wear the banding."

"Yes." He let out a breath. She got the feeling he didn't like taking orders. Or following them.

The doctor turned to her and nodded. "Nice meeting you, Izzy."

"It's nice meeting you, too, Doctor." She'd already forgotten his name. Her mind had been in a thousand places as he walked into the room and introduced himself. The nurse had handed her a writing pad and pen, and Mitch instructed her to sit quietly and think of the orders she had at the shop that needed to be fulfilled. She was grateful for this. And she did need to be organized in her approach to customers. She didn't want to scare them. She wanted them to know that somehow she was going to make sure they received what they'd ordered. Right now, she wasn't sure how that was going to happen, but come hell or high water, it was.

The nurse removed Mitch's IV and the tape that held the wires from the machines. She glanced up once in a while to make sure he wasn't waiting for her. This time, however, when she looked up, he sat on the edge of the bed. The nurse nodded, "I'll step out of the room while you put your shirt on."

Mitch nodded. He lifted his arms to untie the smock they had on him, and he groaned. Izzy jumped up, "Let me help you with that."

She stood before him, reached her arms around his shoulders, and pulled the string to untie his smock. Her cheeks burned hot as she realized how close she was to him. She also realized, she likely smelled horrible after the day she'd had.

She stepped back quickly and turned to the locker across the room. "Is your shirt in here?"

She felt silly and uncomfortable and slightly enamored with the breadth of Mitch's shoulders and the masculine figure he made sitting before her on the bed. She certainly was a mess today.

"I don't know where they put it." He mumbled.

She opened the locker to see a shirt hanging on a

hook, looking worse for wear. There were tears in it, blood on it, and it was dirty. "You can't put this on."

She pulled it out and held it up. She peered through a hole and saw him on the other side.

"It's just till I get home."

"No. I'll be right back."

She stepped quickly from the room and hustled to the gift shop. She could buy him a shirt. It was the least she could do. And she needed to expel some energy anyway.

She navigated the hospital corridors and the elevator to make it to the gift shop. Inside, she found a bright blue t-shirt with a palm tree on it. Across the top of the palm tree, it said, "Blossom Springs, Florida." It would have to do.

She paid more than it was worth, which was typical in hospital gift shops, and hurried back to Mitch's room. Inside, the nurse was giving Mitch his discharge instructions. He looked up when she entered the room, and she smiled. "Here's your shirt."

She handed it over with a grin. He looked at the front of the shirt and smiled. "Perfect."

He groaned slightly as he lifted it over his head, and she rushed to help him. "Here, I can do this." She helped him pull the shirt over his head after he managed to get his arms in the right place, and pulled it down his back. Her fingers grazed his warm skin, and her cheeks burned once more.

As soon as he was pronounced discharged, the

nurse brought the wheelchair to the room. "I don't need to be pushed in a wheelchair."

"It's hospital policy."

"I can walk. Why isn't the policy to let people who can walk, walk?"

The poor nurse, who probably heard this all the time, replied, "I don't make the policy."

A friendly face entered the room. "Mitch, I just heard you were here. How are you, buddy?"

Mitch looked into Mason Thompson's smiling face. "Hey, Doc. I'm fine. A cracked rib and a lump on the back of my head. It's all good."

Mason nodded and glanced at her. "Izzy, are you alright?"

Her cheeks heated, she knew she likely looked simply horrible. "I'm better than I look, I guess." A flood of worry assaulted her as Mason brought back the fact that she had customers who needed their flowers. She'd done the flowers for Mason and Carley's wedding just a few months ago. She struggled to get her breath as the overwhelm covered her like a blanket.

"You actually look like you need to sit down."

Izzy shook her head. "I'm fine. I really need to be making phone calls and arrangements, that's all."

Mason nodded. "If you need anything, Carley and I can help."

She nodded. "Thank you, Mason."

Mitch's voice was gruff when he said, "I need to

contact the hotel owner and get the footage from their place."

Mason nodded. "Yeah. The sooner we find out who did this, the better for everyone. Do you need any assistance?"

"Not yet, but I'll let you know."

She took some slow, calming breaths and closed her eyes for a moment. She would get through this. It would be all right in the end. She couldn't let her father's years of work and toil be lost. Plus, it could have hurt others in the process, which would be hard to overcome.

"Hey." Mitch's voice was soft and raspy. It was actually sexy when he spoke softly. Her eyes flew open and stared into his deep brown eyes.

"You okay?"

Her nose tickled as the threat of tears raged forward from his concern. She sniffed lightly and swallowed the lump in her throat. "Yeah."

He frowned slightly, then nodded. "Let's get out of here, okay?"

"Yeah." She remembered Mason's kind offer of help and turned to see him watching her. "Thank you, Mason. I do appreciate it."

Mason nodded. "I meant it. Let us know."

She nodded and followed the nurse pushing a complaining Mitch in the wheelchair.

Outside, her cheeks grew hotter than the fire that ripped through her sweet little shop. Her pink Petal

Pushers' van was the only transportation she had here to take Mitch home in. She unlocked the van with the key fob, then turned to see him grinning.

"I'm sorry. I had the keys handy for the delivery van and rushed here as soon as the police let me go."

He shook his head slowly. "Don't apologize. I've never ridden in a floral delivery van, so it's a first."

The nurse locked the wheels on the wheelchair and offered to help Mitch stand, which he refused. The stubborn man slowly stood, his jaw clenched tightly as he took a step toward her van. She stood helplessly by as he mulishly managed to seat himself stiffly in the passenger seat of her van. The nurse closed the door and nodded to her. "Call if you need help."

"Thank you. I will."

She moved toward the driver's seat, realizing for the first time that she was a bit sore herself. Nothing like Mitch, of course, but the day's activities were taking their toll.

She started her van and turned her head toward Mitch. "Where do I take you?"

Mitch grinned. "I live in a condo at the Barracks."

"Oh. That's cool."

She put her van in drive and slowly pulled out of the parking lot. She was careful not to jostle Mitch too much; he had to be sore with a cracked rib. After turning right out of the parking lot, she slowly drove toward Main Street. She felt like she could run faster than she was going. But Mitch's comfort was more important than her getting her customer list prepared. She had to keep reminding herself of this.

After a few minutes, Mitch said, "I won't break. You can at least go the speed limit."

"I'm being careful."

"And I do appreciate it, but this is more painful than hitting a bump or two."

She scrunched her nose up, then took a deep breath. "Okay." She sped up to the speed limit, which on this road was thirty miles per hour. Her stress level came down a bit; more to be grateful for.

They pulled into the lot at the Barrack's Condos, and he pointed to a spot toward the end. "I usually park there."

She navigated the lot and parked her van. She quickly hopped from the van and rushed around to the passenger side to help Mitch out.

He had the door open and one foot out of the van when she rounded the side. She stood by helplessly as he scooted and maneuvered himself from the seat. As he began walking toward the door, she was unsure if she should follow him or just go home. She bit her bottom lip as she watched him walk stiffly to the entrance. Then she heard him say, "You coming in?"

"Yes." She shook her head and followed him inside.

Two pool tables were in a common room. There was a long counter and a microwave on it. Some food racks with popcorn bags, packets of salt and pepper, and a few other items were lined up on top. He continued down the hallway. At the end of the hall, he pulled his keys from his slacks pocket and unlocked the door. He pushed it open and stood back to let her enter first.

She stepped into a clean, neatly decorated living room. The large glass window to her left called to her, and as she looked out, she was amazed to see the length of Main Street in front of her.

"What a great view."

"I know. It's what drew me to this place. It also drew Mason here. I bought this from him when he moved in with Carley."

"That's nice." She turned, and the open concept room allowed her to see into the kitchen. With a groan, Mitch sat at the table to the right. His laptop and a small work area were set up near the end.

"If you need something to drink, please help yourself in the fridge."

Moving into the kitchen, she opened the refrigerator and pulled out two bottles of water. She twisted the cap on one, then the other, and took them to the table.

He winced as he leaned over his laptop. He looked pale, tight-lipped, clearly in pain, but stubbornly ignoring it. The soft blue light from the screen washed over his face, highlighting the dark shadows under his eyes.

She swallowed hard, folding her arms as a knot tightened in her stomach. "You should be in bed."

"Could say the same about you," Mitch replied, eyes fixed on the video footage.

He was right. She needed a nap and a hot bath. But her mind wouldn't shut off. Images of her ruined nursery, scorched stems, and shattered windows wouldn't stop looping. Not to mention the guilt.

"I keep thinking about everything," she admitted, moving closer. "The orders I'm going to miss. My dad's legacy. It's all just... falling apart."

Mitch didn't respond right away. Instead, he tapped a few keys and paused a frame. "See that? Someone is moving through the alley. Hood up, face down. Timing's too perfect to be a coincidence."

Izzy squinted. The screen showed a blurry figure barely distinguishable from the surrounding shadows. Her skin prickled.

"That's who did it?"

"Don't know yet. But they were there right before the blast. That's not nothing."

"How do you have that footage?"

"It's from the hotel owners. I texted them on the way home."

"Oh, right."

She took a shaky breath, her fingers twisting together. "I should've told you more before. Things were going wrong for a while."

Mitch finally turned to face her, his gaze steady. "Like what?"

"It started a couple of months ago. Some orchids

disappeared from the front porch. I thought it was teenagers messing around. Then a supplier swore he shipped me a dozen peonies, but they never showed. The tires on my delivery van went flat twice in three weeks. I thought maybe I just needed to be more organized."

Mitch straightened with a wince and grabbed a pen and notepad from the edge of the table. "You should have said something."

"I didn't want to seem paranoid. I'm already the girl with the flower shop on the edge of town, living in her dad's shadow and trying to make it work with lace and dreams."

"Izzy..."

She cut him off, voice trembling. "And now someone's trying to destroy what little I have left."

Mitch's face softened. He didn't speak, just handed her the pen. She blinked, then took it and began listing each incident while he added notes.

Seeing the events written down, one after another, made her stomach churn. "It wasn't just random, was it?"

Mitch tapped the paper. "Looks like sabotage. Whoever it is, they've been escalating."

Izzy nodded slowly, her throat dry. "But who would want to ruin a flower shop?"

He looked back at her, eyes sharp. "That's the question. And I plan to get the answer."

M itch rested his elbows on the table, biting back another wave of pain. The cracked rib was screaming, but he had more important things to worry about. He glanced toward Izzy, who was now pacing the kitchen like a caged animal. She was rattled. Rightfully so. The attack hadn't just torched a flower shop; it had shattered her sense of safety.

"Do you still have the notes?" he asked, nodding toward the list she'd started.

Izzy brought them over, her hands shaking slightly as she handed them off. He skimmed the list. Someone had been messing with her for weeks, maybe longer. This wasn't a random act of vandalism.

"This is deliberate," he said aloud, circling the tire slashing and missing deliveries. "Coordinated."

Izzy sank into the chair across from him. "But why?

I don't have enemies. I sell tulips and sympathy bouquets."

"You also have a storefront on a busy street. Maybe someone wanted it gone. Or maybe it's personal."

She looked at him, eyes wide. "You think someone's targeting me specifically?"

He didn't want to say yes, but she needed honesty more than comfort. "It's possible."

Izzy's gaze dropped to the table. "I can't stay there tonight."

"You're not going back there, period. Not until I figure this out."

"I can stay with my friend Sadie, she and her boyfriend just moved into a house out on First Street. It's nothing fancy, but it should be safe."

Mitch didn't love the idea of her being anywhere without security. But short of chaining her to the chair, he knew better than to argue. "You call her and make sure. I'll follow you over and check the place out myself."

Izzy hesitated. "I don't want you hurting yourself more because of me."

He met her eyes. "I've had worse. And this? This is what I do."

That silenced her. But he saw the slight frown on her pretty face. Even frowning, she was a beauty.

She nodded and pulled her phone from the back pocket of her jeans. While she stepped away to make the call, Mitch turned back to the video feed and rewound it again. The figure in the alley moved with intention. He or she paused for several seconds behind the dumpster, just out of camera range, then slipped off.

That pause bothered him.

Who waits around before setting a fire?

His phone buzzed. A message from Jayson:

> The hotel owner pulled all camera footage from the past week.
> Uploading it to a shared drive now.
> Sending you the link.

Mitch waited for the link, then as soon as it landed in his inbox, he clicked the link and started the download. The sooner he had the full picture, the better.

Izzy returned a few minutes later, stuffing her phone into her bag. "Sadie says yes. Her boyfriend, Trent, is working third shift tonight, so I'll have the guest room."

"I'll need you to drive me to Petal Pushers to retrieve my truck," he said, carefully rising from his seat. He stiffly sauntered to the sofa and, trying to reach behind it, he groaned as stabbing pain ripped through his body.

Izzy rushed to his side. "Let me do that."

"I need my go bag."

"What's in it?"

"Essentials."

He moved to the fireplace in the corner and

touched the side of it where a fingerprint portal was hidden. Slowly, the bottom of the mantle lowered, revealing a few of his many firearms. He picked up his favorite, a Springfield DXM. He also nabbed a couple of loaded magazines and slowly tucked them into his pockets.

Izzy caught sight of the weapons and blinked. "That's an impressive mantle."

He didn't answer at first. Just met her gaze with quiet resolve. "Thanks. It was the first thing I did. I have hidden storage spaces all over this place. I'd rather have my weapons close and not need them than need them and not have them available."

Her throat bobbed in a swallow. "Right."

They rode in silence to her shop. He saw her throat constrict as they neared. Seeing her shop again would be difficult.

"It's special to you, I know." Mitch began. "But it can be rebuilt. Whatever needs to be done can be done."

She nodded and sniffed.

He stared straight ahead and watched the landscape as they neared Petal Pushers. The police crime tape swayed in the breeze.

"Stop here and let me out. I want to walk behind the building to see the path the arsonist took."

"It has police tape around it."

"I'm aware. I'll contact Trey Fielding, Chief of Blossom Springs PD. I work with the police all the time."

He carefully hefted himself from her van. She shut it off and got out of the driver's side. "You need to stay back, Izzy. We don't want to damage any evidence."

"But you might need assistance."

"Stay back, honey."

His heart thumped when 'honey' rolled off his tongue without thought. He shook his head and carefully stepped to the back of the building to investigate the area. The grass had been cut within the past two days, which helped him to see where footprints still showed on the bent grass. He also found a rusty metal cap from an old gas can. He slowly pulled his phone from his pocket, careful not to put too much pressure on his sore ribs. He snapped photos of the cap and texted them to Trey.

> Found this behind Petal Pushers. I have the video footage from the hotel showing someone back here early this morning.

He didn't wait for a response. The sound of a female crying caught his attention, and he turned toward the front of the building.

His heart dropped when he saw a pathetic Izzy Payton standing alone in the debris strewn around her parking lot, staring at the front of her store. The front windows were broken, burnt flowers were wilted into the broken glass, and the sign on the front porch had the name of her shop burnt off, the engraving the only thing telling anyone what the sign once brightly boasted.

He hobbled to her side and took her hand in his. He stood there silently staring at the carnage as Izzy composed herself and took a deep breath. "There, I got that out. Now I can move forward."

His fingers squeezed hers. "That's great. Nice job getting yourself there."

She took a deep breath and turned her head to face him. "Can I go in and see what I can salvage?"

"No. Not until the police remove the tape. They may need to come in and check things out as they uncover evidence. I just sent Trey a picture of a gas can cap that was lying in the back. They'll come back and look further into that."

She blew out a deep breath. "Okay."

He nodded to his truck, which thankfully sat outside of the police tape. "I'll follow you."

"Okay."

He reluctantly let go of her hand and stiffly moved toward his truck. His heart felt weird. Soft or something, and not at all what he was used to. But this pretty little woman, with her own business and a perky demeanor, suffered a huge blow today, and she was handling it like a trooper. And that just had him feeling all soft and mushy. That's all that was. Hopefully, it would be gone tomorrow.

The two-car caravan wound through the quiet backroads of Blossom Springs. Streetlights cast golden glows over the sleepy town. Mitch couldn't shake the feeling that something bigger was brewing.

Izzy pulled into a narrow gravel driveway behind a blue two-story house with flower beds freshly planted. He parked behind her, climbed out slowly, and scanned the property. Dim porch light. One car in the driveway. Curtains drawn. Quiet. Clean.

Sadie greeted them at the door in pajama pants and a baggy college sweatshirt, her arms already open. "Oh my god, Iz, I've been watching the news all day. Are you okay?"

"I'm fine," Izzy replied, though her voice wavered.

Sadie hugged her hard, then glanced at Mitch. "You must be the guy who saved her."

Mitch gave a small nod. "Just doing what needed to be done."

Sadie grinned. "Come in. I got the guest room ready."

He stepped inside behind Sadie and Izzy, and while the women disappeared down the hall, Mitch checked the locks on both doors, peeked out the back window, and mentally mapped the exits. Once he'd checked everything in the front of the house, he moved to the back where the ladies were chatting. He made sure Izzy's room had a window that opened, just in case.

He turned to the women watching him. "This should be good."

She looked more relaxed. "Thanks. For everything."

"I'll be in touch tomorrow," he said. "Don't open the door unless it's someone you know, and text me if anything feels off. Lock the doors after I leave and make sure you listen for anything out of place."

"I will."

Their eyes met again in the quiet of the porch light. Something unspoken passed between them. Worry. Tension. Something else. He shook his head and mentally told himself to get a grip.

Mitch cleared his throat. "We're going to figure this out."

Izzy nodded. "I believe you."

He nodded toward the door and waited until she was safely inside before heading back to his condo. Once there, he downed two pain pills, sank into the couch with his laptop, and started combing through the footage the hotel had sent.

By midnight, he froze the screen on a still image:

A man's silhouette leaning over something behind Petal Pushers.

He zoomed in.

No clear face.

But the bastard had left a clue. Maybe more than the gas can cap. He texted Trey again and asked to meet him there tomorrow.

He was going to find whatever it was.

4

Izzy woke to the soft chirp of birds outside Sadie's guest room window and the faint scent of coffee in the air. For one blissful second, she thought what a wonderful day it would be. Then the incidents of yesterday, the scorched flowers, the charred remains of her dad's shop, assaulted her brain. It all came rushing back. The weight of it felt crushing. Her breathing came in short spurts, and she closed her eyes and told herself to calm down.

She sat up too fast. Her body protested with aches and sore muscles. Nothing serious, just a reminder that yesterday had really happened.

Pushing herself out of bed, she padded into the hallway. Sadie was in the kitchen pouring coffee, wearing the same oversized sweatshirt from the night before.

"You're up," Sadie said gently. "I was just about to come check on you."

Izzy nodded and wrapped her hands around the warm mug her friend handed her. "Thanks. For letting me crash here. For everything."

"Don't mention it." Sadie leaned against the counter, her face lined with worry. "You really okay?"

"No," Izzy admitted, her voice cracking. "But I will be."

They sat in silence at the scarred wooden table in Sadie's cozy kitchen for a few minutes, sipping coffee. The comforting normalcy of the moment helped. But her mind was already spinning. Orders to cancel. Customers to notify. Insurance to call. And then there was Mitch, who'd somehow managed to be both reassuring and frustratingly protective.

Her phone buzzed on the table. A message from him.

Let me know when you're up. I'll come get you, we can go over the footage and talk next steps.

She typed back quickly, with a tingle in her tummy.

I'm up. Give me 30.

Sadie gave her a look. "Was that him?"

Izzy nodded. "He wants to go over the video

footage again. He thinks it might help narrow things down."

Sadie tilted her head. "And what do you think?"

"I think he might be right." She stared into her coffee. "It just doesn't make sense. Who would want to hurt me? Or the shop?"

Sadie frowned. "You ever had trouble with the zoning board or city permits? Anyone complain about your deliveries? Parking?"

"Not really." Izzy rubbed her forehead. "There's that cranky guy behind me, Mr. Hines. He always thought our back deliveries were too loud, but nothing serious. And Delilah Parker's been gunning for the corner shop to expand her nail salon into something more, I think to add clothing, but I thought that was just gossip."

Sadie raised an eyebrow. "Maybe it wasn't."

Izzy blew out a breath. "I don't want to jump to conclusions. But yeah. I guess I'll have to look at everyone a little differently now."

Sadie nodded. "Want help drafting a message for your customers?"

Izzy gave her a tired smile. "God, yes. I don't even know where to start."

Sadie pulled a notepad and pen from a hidden drawer at the table. "I pulled a t-shirt and leggings from my drawer and set them in the bathroom for you. I have a new toothbrush and a travel toothpaste in the drawer. Do you need underwear and a bra?"

"No, I washed mine out in the sink last night and hung them in my room. Thank you."

Sadie smiled, her friend from high school and all her adult life so far, was her rock. "Anything you need, Iz, I'm here."

Izzy's eyes watered. She hugged her bestie tightly, then started toward the bathroom to dress as Sadie began drafting a note to her customers.

After dressing and brushing her teeth, she entered the kitchen, ready for the day, she hoped. Sadie smiled and handed her the notepad. "How about this?"

She read the draft Sadie had put together for a post on Petal Pushers' Facebook and Instagram pages. Sadie kept her tone soft but firm while Izzy made sure the message didn't sound like she was giving up. When it was done, Izzy felt both lighter and raw.

"Once this is posted, it feels like the real work will begin."

Sadie smiled. "I'll help you in any way I can. For instance, should I begin calling your flower vendors and see if they can deliver more flowers to cover your orders?"

"Where will I have them delivered?"

Sadie's pretty lips turned down for a moment. "Ask Jace and Margo at the Sandbar if they have room in that giant house of theirs."

"I only know them from business meetings and having done some weddings and birthday parties there. I'm not really friends with them."

Sadie shrugged. "I'll keep thinking on it."

Her phone buzzed again.

I'm outside when you're ready.

Her heart gave a traitorous little flutter. "He's here."

Sadie gave her a quick hug. "Call me if you need anything. And if you think of anyone suspicious, let me know. I can ask around, too."

"Thanks, Sadie."

She grabbed her purse from the side table in the living room, realizing that Travis' boots were on the rug next to the door. She hadn't even heard him come home. This thought made her nervous, what if someone had been outside trying to hurt her? She'd slept too soundly. She opened the door and stepped outside. Mitch stood beside his truck, leaning slightly on the open door. He looked tired. Pale. But focused.

"You ready?" he asked.

Izzy nodded. "As I'll ever be."

They drove in silence for a few blocks. The kind that wasn't uncomfortable, just... full. She studied his profile, strong jaw, serious eyes, a faint bruise darkening near his temple. He looked like he should be resting, not playing detective.

"You sure you're okay to be doing all this?" she asked quietly.

He didn't look at her. "You're not safe until we find out who did this. So yeah. I'm doing this."

Her heart twisted. "I didn't mean to drag you into my mess."

"You didn't." His voice softened. "But I'm in it now. And I don't walk away from unfinished work."

They arrived at Petal Pushers, and she saw the police squad car already there. Mitch stepped from the truck just as labored as yesterday. He pulled his laptop from the backseat, and she watched his face intently to see if he showed signs of pain. If he was in pain, he was a great actor. If not, he was a miracle.

He set the laptop on the hood of his truck as Trey Fielding approached them.

"Morning, folks."

Mitch shook Trey's hand, and she followed suit. Trey nodded at her, "We'll figure this out, Izzy."

Comfort washed over her. Hopefully, nothing else would happen to anything or anyone. "Thank you."

Mitch pulled the video footage up on his laptop, and the shadowy figure paused on screen.

"That's from about two minutes before the explosion," he said. "They knew exactly where the cameras were. Stayed just out of frame most of the time."

Izzy leaned in. "Can you enhance it?"

He smirked. "You've been watching too many cop shows. It doesn't work like that."

She grinned despite herself. "Had to try."

He clicked through more frames, each one revealing just a fraction of the figure's movement, dark hoodie, slightly hunched shoulders, heavy step.

"See that?" Mitch pointed to the corner of the screen. "That shape, near the dumpster. Could be a gas can."

Her mouth went dry. "So they brought it with them."

"Looks that way."

They sat in silence for a moment, the weight of it all settling over her again.

"What happens now?" she asked.

Trey stepped back. "Stay here, I'll go see if I can find anything besides the lid to the gas can."

He stepped away, and she stood near Mitch as he stared at the computer. He peered around the top of his computer at the hotel behind her building. He began walking toward the corner of the lot line where he could see behind her building and the hotel at the same time. She slowly followed behind him, not saying anything, mostly because she didn't know what to say. He was thinking, and she didn't want to disturb that.

They stopped on the corner, and his eyes tracked the steps the assailant took from the back of the hotel, along the dumpster, to her greenhouse, and then to the back of the building. Trey then stepped from behind the greenhouse, and it startled her. She yelped softly, and Mitch turned to her. He grinned slightly. "He startled me, too. I was so lost in thought for a few moments that I forgot he was back there."

They stood in silence as Trey stared at the ground,

took some photos, and picked up a couple of objects, placing them into baggies for safekeeping.

Mitch took a few photos as they stood there. The nail salon was in front of them and to the right slightly as they stood on the corner of Main Street and Main Square.

"When I chatted with Sadie this morning, I told her I'd heard rumors about Delilah Parker..." She pointed to the nail salon, "Wanting to expand her shop but not having the space here to do it." She swallowed. "I don't want to start anything, it was just a rumor, the way I heard it. But..."

Mitch stared at the nail salon for a while and shrugged. "I'll keep that in the back of my head as we move forward with investigating. I'll talk to Trey and the fire department to see if there's any way I can install cameras today."

"Mitch, in your condition, you should be resting."

"I have help when I need it. And you need cameras. Whoever did this didn't finish the job. It looks as though only the back portion of the building is damaged."

Trey rejoined them. "I found a few small things that may or may not be helpful, but I want to get them back to the department and take a closer look."

Her stomach twisted slightly. "When can I get back inside? I really need to see what's damaged and what isn't and take care of the plants that survived."

Trey nodded. "Let me talk to the fire chief, and I'll let you know."

They watched Trey move toward his squad. Mitch nodded. "Let's get you back home, Izzy."

"I'm not at home." She longingly looked at her precious business and the upstairs where she lived. "I mean I am, but I can't go inside yet."

"You live here?"

She nodded. "It's supposed to be temporary. Until I can find my way clear to buy a little farm out of town so I can grow some of my own flowers and sell them here. Maybe even vegetables."

He turned to look at her. She wore a t-shirt and a pair of leggings that Sadie had loaned her. He smiled. "We'll get you back home as soon as it's safe, I promise."

She nodded. Looking into his eyes, she saw the deep shades of brown and how pretty they actually were. He had thick, dark lashes with slight creases at the corners. He was incredibly handsome. Her tummy fluttered, and she took a deep breath only to inhale his clean, fresh scent. Her heartbeat increased slightly, and she pushed it away and attributed it to thinking it was just all the commotion and gut punch to her life. Nothing more than that.

He opened her door to his truck. She stepped up into it and busied herself with the seatbelt as he hefted himself in without a groan this morning.

As they drove to Sadie's, she asked, "Do you know a place in town where I can have deliveries dropped? If my vendors have the flowers I need, I can still work on fulfilling orders, which will help not only my bottom line, but customer satisfaction too. In the history of Petal Pushers, my father and I have never missed a delivery. I'd love to keep that record, even through all of this."

"I think I do. But let me make a couple of calls first."

"Thank you." She swallowed back the emotion that rushed forward. He was kind, too.

He pulled into Sadie's driveway and turned to her. "You lay low. Rest. Focus on your customers. Let Trey and me figure out the rest."

She wanted to argue. Say she wasn't fragile, that she could handle herself. But the truth was, she was tired. And maybe just this once, letting someone else take the lead wasn't the worst idea.

She gave him a nod. "Okay."

But even as she said it, a tiny voice inside her whispered that if someone had gone to this much trouble to take down Petal Pushers...

They weren't done yet.

Mitch sat at his kitchen table, laptop open, screen frozen on the blurry figure behind the dumpster. His cracked rib throbbed, but he ignored it. Pain he could handle. What he couldn't handle were unanswered questions.

Someone had torched Petal Pushers, and Izzy was inside when it happened. That made it personal. Or careless, but either way, she was in danger, and this should be an attempted murder investigation.

He picked up his phone and dialed Jayson Davis, a former security analyst he served with in the military, and a man who could dig up information faster than most people could blink.

"Mitch. Thought you were done calling in favors."

"I'll be done when people stop setting buildings on fire. I need a background check, Delilah Parker,

Blossom Springs, Florida. Owns the nail salon next to the flower shop that went up yesterday."

"Got it. Give me an hour."

Mitch hung up and scribbled a few notes on a legal pad. The suspect on the footage wasn't just loitering, they'd waited. Calculated. The fire didn't seem like some petty revenge stunt. It was targeted.

A knock at the door interrupted his thoughts.

He opened it to find Trey Fielding holding a brown evidence envelope.

"You alone?" Trey asked.

"Always," Mitch said, stepping aside.

Trey walked in and handed him the envelope. "Partial print on the gas can lid. Nothing conclusive yet, but we're running it through local and state databases."

Mitch opened the envelope and glanced at the photo and debris inside. "Anything else?"

Trey scratched the back of his neck. "Yeah. We canvassed a couple of the local businesses this morning. Talked to Delilah at the salon."

Mitch arched an eyebrow. "And?"

"She was edgy. Claimed she had no plans to expand, but she got jumpy when we asked where she was around 7:30 yesterday morning."

"No alibi?"

"Says she was home. Alone. No one was with her. Said her assistant, Travis, was running some errands for her."

Mitch leaned against the table. "Sadie's boyfriend's name is Travis."

"Yes, one and the same. He does night-time security in town for the feed mill. Odd jobs during the day."

"But this was during a time when he should have been working. Or getting off work, depending on his schedule at the security company."

"Actually, he works directly for the feed mill and not a company. I did a bit of digging. Travis isn't an upstanding sort. He's had trouble with the law before, mostly petty theft and an incident with vandalism and forgery. I have a call into the owner of the feed mill to see if he can shed some light on what Travis' actual responsibilities are."

Mitch nodded. "Okay. And she called Travis her assistant?"

"Yep. That's the title she used."

"And you spoke to Travis?"

Trey grinned. "Said he was visiting his brother in Summerville and didn't see Delilah until later that afternoon."

Mitch frowned. "So they weren't together. And no one can verify where Delilah was. Travis is shady at best."

Trey nodded. "It's thin. But it raises eyebrows."

"Did you contact Travis' brother?"

Trey shook his head, "We're trying to reach him. Haven't yet."

After Trey left, Mitch changed into clean jeans and

a dark DeMario Security short-sleeved tee. He'd already sweat through his morning clothes. Pain clawed up his side as he holstered his Springfield and slid a notebook into his pocket. He was past due for a real rest, but he needed to look Travis in the eye. And he needed to make sure Izzy was safe.

He took a deep breath and seated himself in his truck. Maybe he'd take a short nap today to restore some of his energy. One thought kept running through his mind over and over: Izzy was staying with Sadie in the same house as Travis. If Travis meant her harm, she was directly in his space.

As he pulled into Sadie's driveway, Travis was unloading tools from the back of his truck. The man turned, squinting in the midday sun as Mitch approached him.

"You, Travis?" Mitch asked.

"Yeah. Who are you?"

Mitch pulled a business card from his wallet and handed it to Travis. "Mitch DeMario."

"Oh, you're the person who brought Izzy out here yesterday."

Mitch nodded. "Mind answering a few questions?"

Travis hesitated, then set the tools down. "I've told the police everything."

"I'd like you to tell me too. I don't like hearsay."

Travis took a deep breath and put his hands on his hips. "Fine."

"You do any recent work for Delilah Parker?"

"A week or two ago," Travis replied. "Reinforced her back door, fixed a busted lock, resealed a window."

"So you've been behind her building recently."

Travis crossed his arms. "That's my job. Doesn't mean I set any fires."

"I didn't say you did," Mitch replied calmly. "You just happen to know both women involved, and you were gone when the fire broke out."

"I was in Summerville. My brother and I made a delivery run. He'll vouch."

"Good. I'll be talking to him." Mitch paused. "Ever notice anyone hanging around behind Petal Pushers lately?"

Travis shifted. "There's a guy, beat-up white Chevy, broken taillight, rust around the back wheel. Shows up early. Hoodie, always pulled up. Never delivers anything. Just sits there awhile, then drives off."

"You get a plate?"

"No. Just figured he was waiting for someone."

Mitch made a note. It wasn't much, but it was something.

"Thanks," Mitch said. "If you think of anything else, reach out."

Travis nodded, then pulled more tools from the back of his truck. Mitch watched from the vantage point of his pickup as he pretended to make notes in his notebook. There was a large can in the back of the truck, obscured by tools. He couldn't tell if it was a gas can, and he didn't have a warrant or the authority to force Travis to show him what it was. But he'd let Trey know if Travis turned out to be a suspect.

On his way back to his condo, Mitch's phone buzzed. Jayson's name showed on the readout.

He tapped the answer call icon, "Tell me you've got something."

"Delilah's got two small business loans, both delinquent," Jayson said. "She's on the zoning board's waitlist to expand her shop, but she's been denied three times. Petal Pushers is the reason. She can't grow unless Izzy's shop closes or sells. Or she moves, which she seems reluctant to do."

Mitch rubbed his jaw. "She claims she's not expanding."

"On paper, she's not," Jayson said. "But there's more, her mother tried to buy Petal Pushers years ago. But when Old Man Grady had to get out of it, he sold it to Izzy's dad thirty-five years ago. Word is, Delilah's still bitter about it. Thinks her mom got cheated or some strange thing, even though there's no record of any formal offer made and no record of anything other than Old Man Grady needing the money from the sale of the shop and Izzy's dad buying it."

"So, she's got financial pressure, motive, and a grudge."

"Yep. But no real means. She's broke and her credit's shot. No way she's pulling this off alone."

Mitch's pulse kicked up. "So who is?"

"That's the question. She's been paying someone in

cash, a guy named Rayburn. No job on file. Sketchy background. B&E, arson, theft."

Mitch straightened. "That could be our guy."

"I'll send everything I have."

Mitch hung up and stared at the frozen image on his screen, the hooded figure again, slipping just beyond reach.

Delilah had a motive.

Rayburn had the skill.

And Izzy?

She had a target on her back.

6

Izzy stood in Sadie's kitchen, trying to focus on the list in front of her. Flower orders, delivery requests, invoices, things that had once felt like the rhythm of her life now felt distant and fragile, like petals about to fall.

She rubbed her temple, her heart thudding faster than it should. She'd only slept a few hours the night before, her dreams filled with smoke and shattering glass.

Sadie entered the room, a cup of coffee in each hand. She set one in front of Izzy and sat down opposite her. "You didn't sleep, did you?"

"I tried," Izzy said quietly. "Every time I closed my eyes, I was back in the greenhouse. Hearing the glass crack. Smelling the smoke."

Sadie reached across the table and squeezed her hand. "You're safe now."

But Izzy wasn't so sure. She didn't feel safe. Not even close. She swallowed and took a deep breath. She took a sip of coffee, then looked toward the window. The yard beyond was quiet, but she caught a flicker of movement near the fence. She squinted, heart catching.

Nothing.

Or maybe something. Her shoulders tensed as she continued to stare outside.

"You okay?" Sadie asked, glancing out the same window.

"I thought I saw... I don't know. Something by the fence."

Sadie stood and peered out. "Probably a squirrel. Or Travis. He's always coming and going."

Izzy nodded slowly but didn't feel reassured. She hadn't seen Travis leave this morning, and his truck wasn't in the driveway when she woke up.

"Where is Travis?"

Sadie shrugged. "He does odd jobs to help cover some of his expenses."

"Does he have a lot of them? Expenses, I mean?"

Sadie's shoulders dropped. "I'm finding out more and more. It seems he's been in legal trouble in the past, and he's paying off some of those debts."

Izzy stared into her friend's beautiful blue eyes. While they were always beautiful, today they looked sad.

"Are you alright? Are you happy?"

Sadie shrugged, and her eyes glistened slightly more than they had before. "It's alright." She jumped up and grabbed her keys. "I have to run to the hardware store. Do you want to come?"

"No. I think I need to clear my head. Maybe take a walk. Just around the block."

Sadie frowned. "You sure?"

"Yeah." Izzy forced a smile. "It'll help. I need to do something normal. Waiting for people to call me back is like watching paint dry."

Izzy stood and hugged her friend. "You know you can always tell me everything. Right?"

"I know. Thank you."

She watched Sadie nab her purse off the counter and shuffle to the door. After Sadie left, Izzy laced up her shoes and stepped outside. The morning sun was already hot on her face. She walked down the sidewalk, muscles tight, eyes scanning every corner and parked car.

It wasn't paranoia. It was instinct.

She headed toward town without thinking about what she was doing. She breathed in the heavy, moist air and fresh cut hay as she passed by the Canning Ranch driveway. Though it was long and you couldn't see the house from First Street, the lovely smells of fresh hay and wildflowers they allowed to grow along the fence line were pleasant.

Passing by Carley's real estate office, she smiled as she remembered her wedding just a few months ago, which brought her right back around to the sadness at her circumstance now.

"Get a grip, girl. It could have been so much worse." She squared her shoulders and continued on until she rounded the corner by Main Street and stopped when she saw the front of Petal Pushers. The damage was still roped off with yellow police tape, the windows blackened, the paint blistered. Her stomach twisted.

How many times had she unlocked that front door, arms full of peonies or roses? How many weddings had started with the blooms from that shop? She crossed her arms and tried to breathe through the rising ache in her chest.

"You shouldn't be here."

The deep voice came from behind her. She turned sharply and saw Mitch standing a few feet away, his arms crossed, eyes shadowed by concern.

Her lips curled into a smile. "You always sneak up on people?"

"You're standing in front of a crime scene, looking like a target." He took a step closer. "What if whoever did this came back to make sure it worked?"

"I just wanted to see it again."

He nodded, glancing at the building. "I get it. But next time, bring me."

She looked up at him. He was pale again, sweat starting to bead along his temple.

"You shouldn't be out either," she said. "You look like hell."

"I've been worse."

"You keep saying that."

He gave a faint smile. "I keep meaning it."

She laughed quietly, but the tension between them didn't fade. "You find anything new?"

Mitch's jaw tightened. "Maybe. A guy named Rayburn. Criminal history. Burglary, arson, theft. He's been paid cash by Delilah Parker recently."

Izzy's brows rose. "Delilah? But why?"

"She has no credit. No loans. But she's desperate. She's been denied zoning to expand. Petal Pushers is in her way."

"So you think she hired someone?"

"I think she's hiding something. And Rayburn's got the skills to make this look like an accident."

Izzy folded her arms. "I knew she didn't like me, but I never thought..."

"People don't always do what you expect," Mitch said. "Especially when money and resentment get involved."

She nodded slowly, then turned her gaze back to the building. "I hate that someone did this over property. Over flowers."

He looked at her, his voice softer now. "This isn't just about flowers. It's about what you built. That's what makes you a threat."

She swallowed hard, her eyes burning. "I just want my life back."

He touched her arm gently. "We're going to get it

back. But I need you to be careful. Stay alert. And if you see anything, anything, you call me. Right away."

She nodded. "I will."

A breeze carried the faint scent of smoke still lingering in the air. It clung to the building like a scar.

They stood in silence, both watching it.

Somewhere behind them, a car door slammed.

Mitch turned instantly, hand near his hip.

But it was just a teenager cutting through the alley, earbuds in, oblivious.

Still, Izzy's heart beat faster.

They weren't done.

And neither was whoever had started this.

M itch's phone buzzed on the passenger seat just as he turned onto Main. He grabbed it, thumbed open the text, and read Izzy's short message.

Back at Sadie's. Everything's quiet, for now.

He didn't like that last part, 'for now'. Hopefully it would stay quiet. He replied quickly.

Stay alert and keep me posted.

He pulled into his driveway and parked, wincing as he climbed out of the truck. His rib ached, the muscles in his back were tight, and he hadn't eaten anything more substantial than a granola bar since breakfast.

But his first stop wasn't the kitchen. It was the small gun safe behind the bookshelf.

He unlocked it and pulled out his compact field kit, spare mags, a discreet sidearm, flashlight, and a burner phone. Just in case. He had no hard proof yet, but every bone in his body screamed that something was coming. And Izzy was smack in the middle of it. And somehow, in the blink of an eye, she became important to him. He liked her. Her spunk and her sass, and well, just her.

After running through the latest camera footage and checking in with Jayson, he finally allowed himself a short rest, just twenty minutes to let the meds kick in. He focused on shutting off his mind for a few winks, and finally, his eyelids felt heavy, and he let them close.

The blare of his phone jolted him upright.

He answered on the first ring. "What's wrong?"

Sadie's voice was tight. "Izzy's okay, but someone just tried to get in the back door. She screamed. I called the police. Mitch... it wasn't Travis. He's not here."

Mitch was already grabbing his keys. "I'm on my way. Don't let Izzy out of your sight."

He broke a handful of traffic laws getting across town. When he pulled up in front of Sadie's house, two squad cars were already parked along the curb. He spotted Trey near the side of the house, talking to one of the neighbors.

Izzy stood on the porch, arms wrapped tightly around herself, eyes wide with barely contained fear.

Sadie stood beside her, equally shaken but trying to be strong.

Mitch climbed out of his truck and went straight to her.

She didn't wait. She stepped forward and walked right into his arms.

"I'm okay," she murmured against his chest. "But it scared me so bad. He was right at the door. Rattling it. I thought he was going to come through."

He held her tightly, resting his chin against the top of her head. Her body shook against his, and it created a riot of emotions in him. Anger. Fear for her, and that feeling when you enjoy being with someone. "You did the right thing. You called. You stayed inside."

"I couldn't see him. Just his shape. Hoodie. Tall. That's it."

Trey joined them a moment later. "Whoever it was didn't leave much. No clear prints. A couple of boot scuffs in the mulch. We'll check neighborhood cameras, but it was fast and clean. Like he was testing the response time."

Mitch's jaw clenched. "Escalation."

Trey nodded. "Big time."

Sadie's voice was small. "She can't stay here, Mitch. Not while he's out there. Not with Travis coming and going. I can't keep her safe."

Mitch's jaw tightened. She needed someplace safe. "I can," tumbled from his lips.

Izzy looked up at him, eyes searching his. "I don't want to be a burden."

"You're not."

"Mitch…"

"No more arguing," he said, his voice low but firm. "Pack your things. You're staying with me."

What in the hell was he doing? He needed a safe house. He knew Marco and Theresa had a house that would make a security company jealous. That thought made him grin, and he admitted he was a tad jealous. But he had cameras and safety equipment all around his condo. Cameras outside. Inside pointed to the entry door. And inside his condo, he had alarms, cameras, and weapons. One way or another, she'd be safe at his place until they could figure this out.

Izzy stood stone-still, staring at him. He looked into her eyes. He didn't see anger or distrust. He saw sparkling green eyes, the prettiest shade of green he'd ever seen, staring back at him.

Then, slowly, she nodded.

Sadie gave her a quiet hug. "You'll be okay. I'll check in every day."

"Thanks, Sadie."

She looked into his eyes once more. "I'll follow you in my van."

Her hands were trembling, and her bottom lip quivered. "Leave your van here. We'll come back for it. Plus, it's a large sign to alert anyone and everyone where you are. Not many pink vans around town."

"But what if he damages it?"

"Better it than you."

Her shoulders sank forward, and his heart hurt for her. Things seemed to keep piling on.

He helped her into his truck and saw her glance out the window every few seconds as they drove, like she was expecting the figure in the hoodie to appear in the rearview mirror.

He felt the same way and knew that man was close. He just needed to make a mistake so Mitch or Blossom Springs PD could catch him.

After pulling into his usual parking space at the condo, he pointed up to the corner of the building through his windshield.

"See that camera?"

Izzy craned her neck, then nodded. "Yeah."

"Good. That will capture anyone driving into the parking lot. The span is from that empty building over there..." He pointed to the empty building set aside for Phase Three of the Barrack's plan. "To all the way over there." He pointed to the fence line on the opposite side of them.

"Okay."

He nodded and opened his door. He meant to open hers and help her out of the truck, but she beat him to it and met him on the sidewalk in front of his truck. He still moved slowly. He opened the entry door for her and pointed to the camera above the pool tables. "That camera there is focused on the door."

Izzy looked up at the camera and nodded. He held his hand out toward the hall, and she preceded him to his condo. Before he unlocked the door to his place, he pointed to the corner near the ceiling. "That camera is focused on this door."

"It sure looks like you're prepared."

He grunted. "Yeah. Security and all."

"Right."

He pushed the door open and let her enter before him. "Just past the living room, the door on the left is the spare bedroom. Feel free to take that room. I'm in the one at the end of the hall. The bathroom across from the door to your room is yours."

She nodded. "I do need to get some clothes. Any chance I'll be able to get into my apartment today?"

"I'll call Trey and see if they will allow it and if they think the building is safe."

"Okay.

He pulled his phone from his pocket and dialed Trey's number. He watched Izzy look his place over. She'd already been here briefly, but now she seemed to take more stock in it. She neared the window facing the parking lot and noticed the sensors on the corners. Pride flowed through him as she seemed comforted by his level of security.

Trey answered on the first ring. "Mitch."

"Izzy is wondering if she can get inside her place to get some clothing."

"Yeah. The fire department has cleared the structure for safety. The fire was contained to the very back of the greenhouse. The windows up front had the rocks tossed in, and the Molotov tossed into that window only burned the very front of the inside of the building. It'll take some work to rehab it, but structurally, it's sound. Mostly cosmetic damage."

"Thanks, Trey."

"No problem. I'll keep you posted on any of our findings."

"Roger."

He pocketed his phone and glanced up to see Izzy staring at him. She was a pretty woman. Her long blonde hair was pulled into a ponytail today, but even pulled back, it suited her.

"Trey said you can go in. The building is structurally sound. Are you ready to go now?"

"Yes, please. I'm so anxious to see how much damage there is."

"Okay. Let's go over now."

She nodded and softly padded to the door. Mitch pulled it open and waited for her to pass him. He could smell her fresh scent, and that sent a thrill through his body.

As they exited the vehicle at Petal Pushers, he heard her exhale a deep breath. She was steeling herself for what she was about to see. They both stepped on the front porch, scorched flowers hung from the broken window. The strong smell of burnt wood hung in the air, and the dampness of the wood from the fire hoses emitted an aroma that reminded him of putting out a campfire.

Izzy unlocked the front door and stepped inside. Water covered the floor, and many of the plants had been blown off their display shelves either from the fire or the water hoses. Izzy picked up a few of them and tried standing them up.

"This will take a few days to clean up," she mumbled.

"It will. But we'll find help," he offered.

She turned to him and smiled.

Taking another deep breath, she moved toward a door at the back of the room. "This is the entrance to my apartment."

He followed her up the stairs, grateful his rib didn't bark with every step. The apartment was cute. Decorated in pretty colors, mostly pastels and grays. Everything up here smelled of smoke, and the ash from the fire found its way up, too.

Izzy stood quietly, looking around at the mess, a lone tear tracked down her cheek.

He felt so bad for her; she looked nearly defeated. Then, as if she were a phoenix, she squared her shoulders and took a deep breath. "Okay. I'll gather a few things. I'm afraid they'll need to be washed or I'll be a walking ad for fire protection."

He chuckled, "I have a washer and dryer in the condo, you're welcome to them."

She nodded her head. "Thank you."

She pulled a suitcase from the closet and strode down a short hall to another room, which he assumed was her bedroom. He looked around her cute apartment and the way she decorated it. She had an eye for detail. The picture frames were painted to match the trim work around the doors and windows. She had a mix of older decorative items and newer ones. But they worked together. Design was never something he cared much about. If his condo hadn't already been decorated, it wouldn't have been done by him.

Izzy emerged with a suitcase wheeling behind her. "I think I have most of what I need."

"We can always come back, but please don't come back unless someone is with you. Not until I can get the security cameras set up. I have help coming in the morning."

"Okay."

He slowly leaned down to help her with her suitcase and felt the sharp pain run across his ribs. He froze to breathe it out, and Izzy scolded. "No, you don't. I can do this, you need to heal."

He righted himself and nodded. He hated being unable to do everyday things.

They descended the stairs, and she locked the door to her apartment. She looked around the room. "Do you think I'll be able to come here tomorrow while you're installing cameras and begin cleaning up?"

"I think that's a great idea."

That put a smile on her face, and he was happy for it. She was a beautiful woman all the time, but when she smiled, she was a stunner.

He drove them to Sadie's place to pick up her van and deposited it at the flower shop. Then he drove her home to his place.

"How about we call the Sandbar and order dinner? I'll have it delivered."

"That sounds great. I am getting hungry."

She pulled out her phone and swiped a few times. "I'll have chicken wings in garlic parmesan sauce, please."

He nodded as he dialed the number. It was a speed dial call for him.

Later, when the house was still and the lights were low, he stood in the doorway to her room. She had just showered, and the aroma of her soap hung in the air. His place never smelled so good.

"You need anything?"

She shook her head, voice soft. "No. Just... maybe don't go far."

"I'll be in my room next door. The alarms are set for the night. You're safe here."

"Thank you."

He turned to leave, "Mitch?"

"Yeah." He turned to see her in the dim lamplight of

her room. "Thank you for everything. I don't know how I'll repay you."

He shook his head. "No need for repayment. I want to make sure you're safe. You've become important to me."

Her lips turned up into a soft smile. "You've become important to me, too."

8

I zzy woke to a soft humming sound. For a moment, she didn't remember where she was. Then the scent of Mitch's place hit her: clean linens, a faint trace of his soap, and the rich, earthy aroma of coffee brewing somewhere close by. The window shades were pulled, but there were motion sensors on them, which is what helped her fall asleep last night. More than once, she considered snuggling up against Mitch's strong, firm body, but she thought that was far too forward. He'd think she was slutty. And she didn't want him to think anything like that about her. Mostly because she was not a slut. But his opinion meant a lot.

She sat up slowly. The events of the night before came rushing back: someone trying to break into Sadie's place, the terror, Mitch's arms around her, his promise that she'd be safe here. The feeling that she was safe. The security he had set up more than compensated for any fear she had.

And she believed he meant it. He wanted her to be safe.

She looked around the room. It was simple but comfortable. Pale gray walls and soft lighting. Lifting the window shade, she saw the window framed the tree line outside like a painting. Her suitcase sat by the closet where she had left it. Mitch had even placed a small glass of water and a packet of pain relievers on the nightstand, just in case.

The gesture made her chest ache in the best way. He cared. She hadn't had anyone in her life who'd really cared about her in such a long time. She'd been engaged once, to a man she admired and loved with her whole heart. But he'd broken their engagement and moved to London for his job, without asking her to join him. He just moved on. She was devastated. Then she heard through the grapevine that he'd married about six months after arriving in London, and his new wife worked at the same company as he had. Things started coming together in her mind. Late nights, secret phone calls. He'd been having an affair with this woman, and their company offered them a fresh, clean place to make their relationship permanent. That was five years ago now and Izzy had avoided dating or getting tangled up with anyone since then. When she stepped into her father's place at Petal Pushers, it offered her the diversion she needed to not dwell on her heartache. And she'd fallen in love again, but this time with her flowers and her business. She became happy again on her own. She'd done it for herself. That's why this was so devastating; she'd grown here as an adult. As a woman who'd been broken and cheated on and she'd thrived. No way was she going to let someone take this away from her.

She stretched as she padded around the bed and opened her suitcase on the floor. She pulled on a clean pair of leggings and one of her oversized shirts, then stepped into the hall. The condo was quiet except for the steady tick of the wall clock and the occasional sound of traffic far off in the distance.

She padded toward the kitchen and found Mitch at the table, laptop open, phone to his ear. He had donned a clean gray t-shirt and dark blue sweatpants, and he looked as comfortable as someone with cracked ribs possibly could. His posture told her he wore the rib band he was instructed to wear, and that made her smile. His hair was tousled, and he looked like he hadn't slept much. But he was so handsome. Not only did she feel safe around him, but she liked looking at him. His hair was dark, but there were grays at his temples and stippled throughout. That added to his handsomeness. He looked like a man who had lived a lot of life, but it didn't destroy him.

She looked into his eyes, and he nodded to her, still listening to whoever he was on the phone with.

"Yes, this morning," he said into the phone. "Three

cameras, two motion sensors. I'll install the rest myself."

A pause.

"It has to be first thing. She's going back into her shop, and I don't want her there without coverage. Thanks."

He ended the call and set the phone aside. "Morning."

"Morning," she replied, unsure where to stand. She hovered near the table, twisting her fingers. "You didn't have to sleep on high alert all night for me."

"I didn't. I slept." He raised a brow. "You didn't hear me snore?"

A soft laugh escaped her. "No, thankfully."

He closed the laptop and leaned back in the chair. "How'd you sleep?"

"Better than I expected. Your place... it feels safe."

He nodded once, serious again. "That's the point."

She moved toward the kitchen counter. "Can I make breakfast?"

"You don't have to."

"I want to. It's the least I can do."

Mitch hesitated, then nodded toward the fridge. "Help yourself. Eggs, bacon, make whatever you want. Coffee's made and ready for you. There's bread, too."

She opened the fridge and scanned the contents. "Are you one of those weird people who keeps ketchup next to the eggs?"

"Guilty."

She laughed again and pulled out ingredients, her nerves easing with the rhythm of a simple task. As the bacon sizzled and the smell filled the room, she glanced back at him.

"You weren't kidding about security," she said, nodding toward the tablet propped up next to his laptop. It showed several camera feeds, including the front door, parking lot, and interior hallway.

"I take it seriously," he said. "I've seen what happens when people don't."

The weight behind his words made her pause.

She turned back to the stove. "Mitch... last night. When you said I'd become important to you, did you mean that?"

He didn't answer right away. His chair creaked, and his footfalls, though soft, sounded close to her. She turned as he neared. "I don't say things I don't mean," he said quietly.

Her breath caught.

"Me neither," she managed.

They stood there for a beat, the tension thick, but not uncomfortable. Electric, yes, but safe. Honest.

Then the bacon popped and broke the moment. She smiled and shrugged.

She turned back to cooking breakfast, her heart fluttering like she was sixteen again, and her cheeks heated and likely pink. When they sat down to eat a few minutes later, it felt oddly domestic. Like a routine they'd done a dozen times.

Halfway through breakfast, Mitch's phone buzzed. He glanced at the screen and his expression hardened.

She set her fork on her plate and waited, trying to remember to breathe. It wasn't any of her business what this message was about, but curiosity coursed through her. And of course, since he was heavily ingrained in her protection, and the scowl on his face, she worried it wasn't good news, and it affected her.

He looked up at her. "Rayburn was spotted in Summerville this morning. Near the edge of town. He matches the build of the man who came to the house last night."

Her spine stiffened, and she sat up straighter. "He's still nearby?"

"Which means we're close," Mitch said. "And he's getting desperate."

She swallowed hard. "I don't know how to feel about that. What should I do with this knowledge?"

Mitch reached across the table and took her hand. His grip was warm, steady, and strong.

"We stay smart. We stay alert. And we don't let him win."

Her heartbeat increased, and she had a hard time swallowing. She was safe here, but that man, a man she didn't even know, was after her for some reason. It seemed so implausible that Delilah Parker would stoop to something so dirty for property.

Mitch stared at her for a long time. "You're safe here."

"I know. I just can't get past the fact that Delilah would be willing to kill me for my shop. If I die, she won't have the chance to get it. It goes to my sister, Iris, who lives in Georgia. And Delilah doesn't have the money to buy it from her. So I honestly don't understand the game plan."

"Sometimes these things don't have a reasonable explanation. And we aren't sure it's Delilah, though no other suspect has shown themselves yet."

"Right." She took a deep breath and stood from the table. Setting her plate in the dishwasher, she busied herself with kitchen tasks. Clearing the table, rinsing the dishes and placing them in the dishwasher, all things to keep her busy.

Mitch stiffly stood from the table. "I'm going in to take a shower and get ready to meet, Jayson, my employee, to help me out with the installation of your security system. You're welcome to stay here while we install."

"No. I'd like to go and begin cleaning things up."

He nodded. Then he smiled at her, and her heartbeat went wild. Handsome. He was incredibly handsome. And her cheeks heated as she stared at his lips and wondered what they'd feel like against hers.

9

M itch stepped under the hot spray and exhaled slowly, letting the water loosen the tension riding high in his shoulders and the soreness in his ribs. They still ached, the tight bandage barely keeping the pain at bay, but it was nothing compared to the heaviness in his chest.

Izzy.

He hadn't expected her to get under his skin so fast. But there she was, tugging at him with every word, every look, every damn breath she took. Last night, she'd curled up in his guest bed like she finally let herself exhale. This morning, she stood in his kitchen like she belonged there. Like this was normal.

He hadn't realized how much he missed normal until now. His heart ached again, and he resisted the urge to rethink his past and the mistakes he'd made, but he failed. The relationships he could have had but chose to ignore because he didn't want to be tied down. His life in the military had been filled with friends and occasional one-nighters. That was less messy. Less anchoring. He could put in for a transfer when he wanted. If a great job assignment came his way, he took it without having to clear it with someone else. He'd liked it that way. But now, it seemed lonely and self-centered. He'd met women in his life he thought he could make a life with, but then he'd hear of a friend divorcing, or a bad breakup, especially in the military, transfers happened on the regular. Shit happened, and frankly, the things they saw changed a person. He never wanted to bring that shit home to someone else. His father used to say, "A strong man deals with his shit on his own. You don't bring shit home to your family." In Mitch's mind, it was simply easier not to have a family. His brothers, Dakin and Austin, had a marriage and a divorce each. He'd talked them through the harsh times, and he always thought – that's not for me.

He turned off the water, dried off quickly, and tugged on jeans and a fresh T-shirt. His movements were stiff, and the rib wrap dug into his side, but the adrenaline of the morning and the coming work dulled the edge. Rayburn was near. That meant things were about to escalate, and he needed to be ready.

When he stepped back into the main room, Izzy was already dressed and waiting by the door. Her hair was pulled into a loose bun, and a purse was slung over one shoulder. Her eyes met his, and there was a flicker of hesitation, concern, maybe, but she didn't voice it. And he realized just how strong this woman was. Sure, she'd shed a few tears. Who wouldn't? But here she stood, knowing someone was after her and still more worried about her customers than herself. She wasn't self-centered. He didn't deserve to be with someone as good as she was. They were polar opposites.

She said, "You sure you're okay to do this today?"

He grabbed his keys from the drawer near the door and offered her a small smile. "I've done worse with less."

"That's not comforting," she muttered.

He chuckled. "Come on. Jayson's meeting us there. We'll get it done fast."

They rode in silence for a few blocks. Mitch kept his eyes moving, scanning every alley, every driveway, every unfamiliar car. Izzy did the same. Rayburn's rap sheet said he had experience. If he'd been at Sadie's last night, he might be watching for another opportunity. Mitch hoped by leaving Izzy's van at the shop, Rayburn would think she was there and make a mistake or question where she was and hang around, which would be a mistake. Either way, it gave Mitch a slight edge. Never pass up an edge.

When they pulled up to Petal Pushers, Jayson was

already there. He leaned against his work van with a coffee in hand and a tool belt slung low on his hips. He was watching the town square across the street from Petal Pushers.

"Hey, boss," Jayson called out. "Got everything we need right here."

"Morning." Mitch climbed out, moving slower than he liked. "Let's make it quick. Cameras first, then sensors. Full perimeter. Inside and out."

Izzy came to stand at Mitch's side. "Izzy, this is Jayson. He's the man I told you about who can find minutiae in anything, including people. He's also one of my installers and very good at his job."

Izzy's smile was brilliant. "It's nice to meet you." She held her hand out to shake Jayson's.

Jayson grinned as he shook Izzy's hand. "Nice to meet you, too. Mitch has mentioned you."

Izzy's head turned to his. Their eyes locked and her lips turned up in a beguiling smile. "You have?"

Mitch shrugged. "In passing."

Jayson chuckled. "I'll get to work."

Inside the shop, Izzy immediately went to work. She started gathering debris and glass from the floor near the back door. The water had largely evaporated, but there were small puddles here and there. The humidity in the air was thick, though it wasn't much less humid outside. Mitch watched her for a moment. She moved like she needed the distraction, like stillness might swallow her whole. But she focused on her work, tossing the glass into a wastebasket and checking on the plants. She began moving them into sections within the building with purpose, and he admired how she cared for her plants and how she knew what needed to be done.

After admiring her for a moment, he set to work with Jayson, and together they began drilling, wiring, and mounting cameras. Each new angle covered blind spots Mitch had mentally mapped out the day he first walked through the shop.

The sweat dripped from his temples. While Izzy had the air-conditioning on in the building, the humidity clung to him. That and the occasional tug and pull in his ribs. Often it shot a sharp pain through him as he bent or twisted in the wrong way. His teeth clenched together more than once.

As they finished mounting the last interior camera, Mitch caught movement outside the shop window. A man stood across the street looking at this building. He had a ball cap pulled low over his eyes. His hands were in his pockets. He wore a black t-shirt and jeans. Black tennis shoes. That was an unusual color this time of year, and especially when it was so ungodly hot out. But the staring is what caught his attention.

His gut tensed. He glanced around to see where Izzy was in the shop. There wasn't any way that man could see in from that distance.

"Mitch?" Izzy's voice was soft behind him.

He didn't answer right away. He watched the man for a beat longer until the guy turned and walked off toward the post office. It could've been nothing. But his instincts screamed otherwise.

He turned to her. "Stay inside. Lock the front door."

She frowned. "Why? Did you see something?"

"Maybe. Let's be cautious."

Jayson reappeared from the back. "That's it. Everything's live. You'll get alerts on the app. Same log-in we talked about this morning."

"Good work," Mitch said. "Grab the spare unit from the truck and wire the window sensors. I'll finish up here."

Jayson nodded and headed out.

Mitch turned back to Izzy, lowering his voice. "This isn't just about covering ground anymore. It's about closing in. He may be watching us, Izzy."

Her breath caught. "I still don't understand."

"I don't either. But we're going to find out."

He stepped closer, lowering his voice further. "I need you to trust me. Completely. If I tell you to leave, you leave. If I say we stay low, we do. I don't want anything happening to you because I underestimated this guy."

She nodded once. "I trust you."

The words sank into him deeper than he expected. That kind of trust was earned, not given. And she was offering it freely.

A moment passed between them, quiet, heavy with something unspoken. He enjoyed staring into her eyes. The color of fresh grass was his new favorite color. Her throat constricted as she swallowed. He wanted to lean in and kiss her.

Then the front door chimed.

Mitch spun, body tense, hand instinctively going to his waistband.

But it was just a deliveryman. Floral supply drop. Routine.

Izzy greeted him. "Hi, Noah. Thank you for making this delivery on such short notice. Can you bring it around back?"

"Wow, you weren't kidding when you said you had some damage."

"Yeah." Her voice was softer than normal, and he watched to make sure she wasn't going to cry. She didn't. She smiled at the delivery driver, signed the receipt, and handed him the clipboard. "I'll meet you back there and make room for this shipment."

"Sounds good. I'll be there in a minute."

Mitch didn't relax until the guy left. Even then, he was coming back in. Izzy seemed to know this guy, so it wasn't Rayburn disguising himself. He'd still be watching every move, though. People could be bought, he knew that from past experience. He'd had a job once as a security detail for a politician. It was a temporary, easy gig. Follow this guy around on the campaign trail and make sure no one got too close.

Easy. Until it wasn't. Turned out, the person organizing the campaign stops was paid a hefty sum to share the routes and hotels where the hopeful congressman was staying. He was shot as he exited the hotel one morning, and Mitch never saw it coming. He'd never make that mistake again.

10

Izzy wiped her hands on her apron and stepped into the back hallway just as Noah pushed the dolly through the door, stacked high with fresh flower buckets.

"Perfect timing," she said, holding the door open wider. "You can park those next to the cooler."

"You got it," he replied, his voice its usual easy tone. "Hot one out there today."

She chuckled. "Feels like walking into a bowl of soup." She moved aside to make room.

Noah maneuvered the dolly with practiced ease, humming under his breath as he unloaded the flowers. Noah had been delivering to her for almost two years now, and she enjoyed chatting with him. She signed the form and handed it back.

"Appreciate you," he said, tucking the clipboard under his arm.

"Thanks, Noah. I'll see you Thursday?"

"Yep."

He rolled the dolly out the back door, and she returned to the shop floor, checking her phone. One missed call from a carnation wholesaler. She made a mental note to return the call once the install was finished.

Mitch stood near the front, watching Jayson finish wiring the motion sensor above the door. The crease between his brows hadn't eased all morning. He kept scanning outside like he expected someone to pop out from behind a mailbox.

She moved toward him, brushing her hand lightly against his arm. "Everything okay?"

"Just keeping an eye out," he said, his voice low. "I'm going to walk the perimeter once Jayson finishes. We only have the back door sensor left to go."

Jayson climbed down from the ladder and nodded to Mitch. "Does that one show up on the computer?"

Mitch checked the tablet he held. "Yep. Rattle the door."

Jayson twisted the handle and tugged on the door. The tablet flashed a red warning, and the camera that was pointed at the front door zoomed in on the door. Mitch grinned. "It's working."

Jayson closed the ladder and moved to the back door. Both she and Mitch followed him. It was interesting watching this process. And she enjoyed watching Mitch at work. She'd been watching him at work at the condo, but here in her space, in her little shop, she enjoyed watching him interact with Jayson and his attention to the job Jayson was doing. Plus, she'd be lying if she didn't admit it made her feel better to know he was ensuring everything was installed correctly.

As Jayson opened the back door to glance around the framework and trim to hide wires, she noticed Noah's truck drive slowly down Main Street, which was to the right of her shop, as she was on the corner. But what caught her attention was Noah pulling into Delilah's parking lot.

She watched as Noah pulled to the side of the building, exited his truck, and then entered Delilah's from the back.

Her stomach sank. She blinked, unsure at first what she had just seen. "That's weird."

Mitch followed her line of sight. "What is?"

"That was Noah," she said. "He just went into Delilah's building. Through the back."

Mitch didn't speak right away. He moved to the side window for a better angle, but Noah was already out of sight.

"You sure it was him?" Mitch asked.

"One hundred percent." Izzy nodded. "He just left here a few minutes ago."

Mitch's expression darkened. "Have you ever known him to do that before?"

"Never." She took a breath, worried she might be

getting Noah in trouble for something. "Of course, I've never watched where he went after he left here."

She couldn't explain the knot forming in her chest. It wasn't just the odd timing. It was how casual it had seemed. Like Noah had done it before. He didn't knock or wait to be let in; he entered on his own.

"Could be nothing," Mitch said, but his voice lacked conviction.

"Could be," she echoed, though her skin prickled in warning.

He looked at her again, more serious now. "I'll check into it. Quietly."

She nodded, heart thudding against her ribs. She didn't want to jump to conclusions. Noah had always been kind. Dependable. But if he was connected to Delilah in any way, she needed to know.

"I don't want to believe he's involved," she said quietly.

"I know," Mitch replied. "But if she's using people to watch you, we can't afford to ignore anything."

The rest of the afternoon passed in a haze of tension. Izzy kept her hands busy, moving flowers to the cooler, repotting new arrivals, checking on her inventory system, rearranging what little product hadn't been damaged, and sadly, taking pictures and tossing out the flowers she lost. Her insurance company told her she had to do that. But her thoughts kept drifting back to that moment. To the look of familiarity in Noah's steps as he disappeared into Delilah's office.

And the way Mitch's entire demeanor had shifted was weird, too. But he wasn't sharing his feelings on what he thought was going on. The most worrisome feeling right now was that the tempo in her cute little shop had changed. Mitch was tense. Jayson was tense, too. They whispered to each other now, where previously they'd spoken out loud.

Something was wrong. She felt it now in her bones.

And this time, she was sure she wasn't imagining it.

The bell above the door rang, and something on the computer screen Mitch held buzzed. Still reeling from Mitch thinking he saw something, she cautiously turned, praying it was someone friendly and not suspicious coming in. Her eyes widened as her friend, Sadie, smiled from the doorway.

"I thought I'd come down and see if you need help cleaning."

Izzy's heartbeat fluttered, and she quickly shortened the distance between her and Sadie. "I'd love your help. It's so nice to see you."

Sadie hugged her warmly, then pulled back and smiled. "I'm always here for you. Put me to work, what do you need from me?"

Mitch stood at the edge of Izzy's workbench, one eye on the tablet displaying the five camera feeds, the other on the shop door. Jayson had finished wiring the last motion sensor and was now organizing cables into a labeled case, but Mitch's focus was elsewhere.

Noah.

Mitch had caught only a glimpse of him heading into Delilah's back door, but that glimpse had flipped something in his gut. A quiet alert. A shift in instinct. The easy-going delivery guy suddenly looked a little too casual, sliding into the back of a salon that had nothing to do with flower deliveries.

He didn't want to say anything to Izzy yet, not more than he already had. She was already trying to keep it together, torn between suspicion and loyalty. And he didn't blame her. From what he'd seen, Noah was professional, and Izzy said reliable.

Which made it worse. For her.

Mitch waited until Izzy stepped into the back room to email her insurance inventory photos before stepping outside to talk to Jayson.

"You got a second?" Mitch asked when Jayson turned toward him.

"Always. What's up?"

"I need a background pull on a guy. Noah Grady. Works for SunnySide Floral Delivery. Drives a white delivery truck. Been delivering to Petal Pushers for almost two years."

"Got it," Jayson said, tapping on his laptop. "This about the fire?"

"Maybe. Just spotted him entering Delilah Parker's place through the back door. No knock, no hesitation."

Jayson let out a low whistle. "That's not nothing. Hang on."

Mitch waited, watching the alley beside the building, every car that passed by, every shadow that moved too quickly. He watched a dog run behind the building. Birds swooped low, catching bugs, and a slight breeze swirled the scent of burnt wood, flowers, and the honeysuckle blooming nearby.

After a minute, Jayson came back on the line. "Okay. Noah Grady. Clean record. No arrests. Former Army Reserves, honorable discharge. Been delivering for Sunnyside for three years, no complaints. But…"

Mitch straightened. "But?"

"He's listed as a contractor, not an employee. Which means he owns his delivery route and contracts with multiple clients."

"Could Delilah be one of them?"

"Officially? No records. But if she paid him under the table or with personal checks, it wouldn't show up unless we dig deeper. Want me to go that route?"

"Yeah. Quietly. I don't want to spook him."

"You got it. I'll run it through alternate databases, look for connections. Do you think flowers are the only thing he delivers?"

Mitch's nose twitched, and his jaw clenched. "I don't know."

"I'll see if I can find any other connection."

Mitch ended the call and leaned against the side of the building. A breeze stirred his shirt, sticking damp fabric to his ribs. He closed his eyes for a moment, trying to center himself.

It wasn't just that Noah might be involved.

It was that whoever was behind this knew how to hide. Knew how to use people who didn't look like threats.

And it was starting to piss him off.

He headed back inside, where Izzy was kneeling in front of the cooler, wiping down the chrome trim. She looked up when he entered, her eyes holding the question she wasn't ready to ask again.

He gave her a small nod to signal everything was fine for now.

Jayson entered a second later and handed Mitch a USB drive. "Backups are saved. If someone yanks your internet or damages the hub, you've still got copies."

"Thanks." Mitch pocketed the drive. "Appreciate the fast work."

"No problem. Want me to run another perimeter sweep?"

"Not yet. Take a break. I might have another task for you if this lead pans out."

Jayson nodded. He was good like that. Trusted Mitch's instincts and knew when to hold questions.

As the afternoon dragged on, Mitch remained in the front of the store, watching. Not just the doors or the footage. He was watching patterns. Watching Izzy. Watching the way her hands slowed when she caught sight of the sidewalk. How her expression dimmed every time a delivery truck passed by.

This was what the fire starter wanted: fear, chaos, disruption.

And he was done playing defense.

When the shop finally quieted, Mitch stepped beside Izzy as she cleaned off a damaged display shelf.

"I'm going to follow up on something tonight. Quietly. I need you to stay at the condo. Keep the alarm armed. Jayson's going to monitor the live feeds remotely."

Izzy looked at him, hesitant. "What are you following up on?"

He didn't want to lie. But he also didn't want to make her doubt everyone she'd ever trusted.

"Noah's name came up again. I just want to see where the trail leads."

She swallowed hard but nodded. "Okay."

Mitch reached out and tucked a loose strand of hair behind her ear. "I won't do anything risky. Just observing. But I'd like you to keep your delivery van and your car here in the garage. I don't want you stranded, but if the culprit doesn't know where you are, you're safer."

She nodded slowly. "Just... be careful."

He nodded once. "Always."

But as they left the shop an hour later, slipping through the back alley to where he'd parked under the shade, Mitch felt that thrum in his chest again. That cold, calculated calm he hadn't felt since his last assignment overseas.

He helped Izzy into the passenger seat and hurried around his truck. He eased from the back of Izzy's greenhouse and onto Alley Drive, just behind the shop. They both looked closer at Delilah's place as they drove away. He'd watched Noah's truck pull away from the shop about a half an hour after he arrived. There wasn't anyone there now. Not even Delilah's vehicle.

This wasn't just about fire or sabotage anymore.

Someone had gotten too close to Izzy.

And Mitch was going to get to the bottom of it, one quiet step at a time.

He walked close to Izzy as they entered the Barrack's Condos and stepped quietly down the hall to his place. He opened the door and made a mental note to have a key made for Izzy. She'd likely feel like a prisoner here tonight. Alone, scared, worried. That sat like a hot rock in his stomach, but there was no way around it. He needed to do this. It was his job, and since people could be encouraged or paid to do simple things for others, he wasn't risking that one of his employees would be approached and enticed. Though he'd fire anyone on the spot and kick their asses out the door at the same time if he found out anyone would betray him, his clients, or anyone close to them.

He closed the door and watched Izzy for a few moments. "I'll be home before eleven, maybe sooner. I'll call or text when I'm on my way so you aren't surprised. Make yourself at home. Watch a movie or read or whatever you like to do. Just, please, don't leave the condo. Not even to go down and shoot pool. Stay inside this condo where you're safe. I can see anyone approaching on my phone from the cameras."

She bit her bottom lip. "Okay. It should be easy, I'm exhausted after all the cleaning today. I'll simply take a shower and huddle in my room or something."

"Sounds good. Don't forget to eat."

"What about you? You need to eat too."

He grinned. "I'll grab something I can eat while I'm driving. Tomorrow we'll eat together."

He saw her throat constrict as she swallowed, and his stomach twisted slightly. Poor girl.

He leaned down and kissed her lips softly. They felt perfect against his. Soft and pliable. This close, he could still faintly smell her shower soap from this morning, though it was masked slightly with the smoky air and dirt she'd been mired in all day. Both of them had been mired in.

His right hand slipped behind her head and held her in place as he deepened the kiss. Her soft, warm tongue slipped along his, slowly, sensually, and his heartbeat quickened. Izzy stepped closer to him and her breasts rubbed against his chest. His breathing hitched as his mind whirled, trying to keep up with all of the emotions running through him. Today alone, he had more emotions than a teenage girl, and his head, no man's head, was capable of processing that.

He reluctantly pulled his lips away from hers, and he heard her sigh. He kissed her forehead and let the air from his lungs. When he spoke, his voice cracked. "Go take a shower and get something to eat. I'll be home as soon as I can."

She stepped back and looked into his eyes. Hers were incredibly beautiful. Green and clear, even after the day she'd had. Her lips tipped up in a soft smile, and he stepped back or he'd forget himself here in a moment.

"I'll be back soon."

He turned quickly and strode to the door. He twisted the deadbolt into place with his key after stepping into the hallway. As he hustled to his truck, he swallowed to moisten his throat. Things were getting jumbled up. This stopped being a job. When had that happened? It seemed like the instant he'd met her.

As he hopped into his truck, he noticed she'd pulled the blinds in the front window. It made him smile, she was smart and listening, and being cautious. He chuckled as he pulled from his parking spot and headed toward town.

Mitch sat in his truck a half block down from Delilah Parker's salon, engine off, lights dimmed, and interior cloaked in darkness. The humid Florida night pressed against the windows, and the cicadas buzzed like static. He sipped slowly from a lukewarm bottle of water and adjusted the long-lens camera resting in his lap.

Noah's truck was parked at the side of the salon again. Same spot. No signage. No deliveries visible.

Mitch checked the time, 9:42 p.m. Way too late for a floral delivery. Actually, way too late for any delivery. Delilah's place had been dark when he arrived just before nine, but ten minutes later, a faint glow appeared in a rear window. Now a second vehicle, a dark gray SUV, had backed in beside Noah's truck.

He snapped a few photos and lowered the lens. His gut tightened again. Noah hadn't looked like a guy wrapped up in anything serious. But criminals rarely wore labels. And Delilah... she had the perfect setup for side dealings: a high-traffic business, private back entrance, and shaky finances.

Mitch jotted a note in his log and leaned back, letting the shadows swallow his truck. He thought of Izzy, safe in his condo, the security system armed, Jayson monitoring the feeds from his place. She'd done everything he asked, and now it was his turn to deliver answers.

Movement.

Noah emerged from the building, holding what looked like a plastic tote in both hands. Not flowers. No logo. He carried it like it had weight. He opened the back of the SUV, stashed the container inside, and exchanged a few words with the driver, a man Mitch couldn't identify in the dark. They didn't shake hands. No smiles. Strictly business.

Mitch reached for his phone and sent a silent text to Jayson.

Noah just transferred something from Delilah's to a gray SUV. No visible tags. Getting footage.

Then another photo, zoomed in. Fuzzy, but legible enough.

A second tote appeared. Another quiet exchange. Then both men climbed into their respective vehicles. The SUV turned out first, heading east on Main Street.

Mitch slid down in his seat as the SUV passed his parking spot near the Craft Mall. The SUV then turned left onto Hospital Road and a quick right on First Street, before disappearing into the night.

Noah lingered.

That's when Mitch saw it.

Noah stepped back toward the door, unlocked it, and went inside.

Why go back in? And he had a key?

Mitch's instincts kicked in harder now. He watched, waited, and prepared to follow if needed. He'd already memorized multiple exit routes, and the tiny camera suctioned to his dash was recording every frame.

Ten minutes passed.

Then fifteen.

Finally, Noah reappeared, locking the door behind him. He glanced up and down the alley, once, twice, then he looked down Main Street before he climbed into his truck and pulled out, heading east out of town.

Mitch let a beat pass, then started his truck and followed.

Noah didn't drive like someone being followed, steady speed, full stops, no glances in the mirror. Mitch stayed back several car lengths, using side streets and a quick turn to cut through a vacant lot and meet him on the next stretch of road.

He trailed him all the way to an industrial strip just outside of Summerville. Noah pulled into a warehouse with no markings, backed into the side of a corrugated steel building, and killed the lights. He didn't unload anything. Just sat there.

Waiting.

Another car pulled up. This one Mitch didn't recognize, a beat-up sedan with tinted windows and a rattling muffler.

This wasn't a floral delivery. This was a drop zone.

And Mitch had just confirmed Noah Grady was more than a delivery guy.

He picked up his phone again.

> Got footage. Multiple transfers.
> Suspected product drop at warehouse
> off Route 12. I'm staying put until I ID
> the buyer.

He thought about Izzy again. Her smile. The way her voice wavered when she said she didn't want to believe Noah was involved.

Neither did Mitch. For her sake.

But belief had nothing to do with facts. And tonight, the facts were stacking up in all the wrong directions.

He settled back in his seat, camera in hand.

He'd stay until he had answers.

Or until someone gave him a reason to act.

Izzy curled her legs beneath her on the sofa, her fingers loosely wrapped around a mug of tea she hadn't touched in over twenty minutes. The condo was quiet except for the hum of the fridge and the occasional creak of the air conditioning kicking on. Too quiet. Too still. It only made her thoughts louder.

She'd double-checked the locks. Armed the security system. Pulled the blinds. Then checked the locks again, just to be sure. Mitch's place was clean and modern, with just enough warmth to feel lived in, but tonight, it felt like a fortress, and she wasn't sure if that comforted or unsettled her. But every time she thought about how Mitch's lips felt against hers, she heated up and had to walk around the condo to expel energy. Forcefully changing her thoughts to other things so she didn't read too much into anything. They'd only met a few days ago, and while he was incredibly attractive, she'd read enough books to know that women always fell for their protectors. It was impossible not to. They were bigger than life and made them feel safe and secure. Who doesn't want to feel safe and cared for?

She shook her head to change her thought trajectory once more. And her thoughts turned to Noah. He'd always seemed polite. Consistent. Helpful. And then, there he was, slipping into Delilah's place like it was no big deal. Like he belonged there. The memory twisted in her chest.

She took a deep breath and tried to focus on something else. Mitch had told her to eat, so she had. Barely. Half a sandwich and a handful of grapes. Now, she was just... waiting.

Her phone buzzed on the end table, and she jumped.

On my way back. Be there in 15.

– Mitch

She exhaled hard, relief washing through her. He was safe. He was coming home. Then that thought stopped her dead. Home, as if they shared this space. Their home. They didn't share this space. Well, they did and they didn't. It was temporary. Until he found the person trying to harm her.

She padded into the kitchen, rinsed her mug, and then wandered into the bathroom to freshen up. By the time she heard the lock disengage, she was already halfway to the door, her pulse ticking a little faster.

Mitch stepped inside, looking tired but alert. His eyes found her immediately and softened a fraction.

"You're okay," she said, her voice quiet but steady.

"I'm okay." He locked the door behind him. "You did everything right. Thank you. It gave me the ability to focus on what I needed to focus on and not worry about whether you were safe."

She reached for him without thinking, wrapping her arms around his middle. He didn't hesitate; his arms circled her tightly. His warmth, his scent, wood smoke, and citrus. Mitch grounded her in a way nothing else had all evening. She closed her eyes as she rested her head against his chest. The steady thrum of his heartbeat and the solid wall of his chest felt like a balm on an open wound.

He pressed a kiss to her hair and held her a beat longer before pulling back just enough to see her face. "It's not good."

Her stomach sank. "Noah?"

He nodded grimly. "Caught him making a drop at Delilah's outside to a vehicle. No flower crates. Just unmarked bins. Then he met with someone else at a warehouse outside of town. Different car. Different exchange."

Her breath hitched. "So it's real. He's really involved."

"It looks like he's involved in something, what that

is, I don't know. I have it all recorded. Jayson's working his end, but I've got visuals. Depending on whether Jayson can find out who the plates of the two vehicles belong to may help us ferret out what Noah is up to."

Izzy leaned back against the counter, and her knees shook. "What happens now?"

"Now, we keep you safe. And we tighten the circle. I'm not sure what exactly he's moving or who it's for, but it's not flowers or floral supplies. And it's not legal, or it would be done during the day and not in an empty lot outside of town."

She nodded slowly, pressing a palm to her chest like that would settle her spiraling thoughts. "I trusted him."

"I know." Mitch stepped closer, brushing a hand along her arm. "But that's not your fault. He was good at hiding it. And, to be completely honest, we don't know it was Noah who started the fire. All I know right now is that he is involved in something that seems outside of the law, and he knows Delilah."

She blinked back sudden tears. "I don't know who to trust anymore."

"You can trust me," he said softly. "Always."

And in his eyes, she believed it. The deep brown depths of his eyes, the sure way he looked at her, the lengths he was going to keep her safe, all spoke volumes to his honesty and his level of trust.

She gave him a shaky smile. "You hungry?"

"I could eat."

She turned toward the fridge, grateful for something normal to do. "Let me heat up some of the lasagna you have in the fridge. Tomorrow I'll make something fresh for you. You can fill me in while you eat."

He reached for her hand before she could move. "After that... I'd like to kiss you again."

She smiled as her whole body tingled. Yeah, she'd like to kiss him again, too.

She nodded once. "Deal."

She moved to the kitchen, knowing he was watching her. Closing her eyes for a moment as she opened the refrigerator, she took a deep breath. It didn't matter that this was temporary, did it? They were attracted to each other, and why couldn't they explore that? It's not like either of them was a virgin. They were consenting adults. Right?

Mitch sat at the table as Izzy warmed his dinner. He yawned, the fatigue from the day finally catching up to him. While he had more information, he didn't feel any closer to an answer or a solution for Izzy's problem. First thing in the morning, he'd call Blossom Springs PD and see if they had any more information from the items they'd found.

Izzy brought a plate of hot lasagna, steaming from the microwave, and set it in front of him. She turned to the refrigerator and brought both of them a beer. She popped the top off of them. He grinned and held his beer up toward her. She smiled sweetly as she tapped her bottle to his. He took a long drink from his bottle and enjoyed the feeling as it slid down his throat. She sat at the table across from him.

"Ahh, that tastes fantastic."

She chuckled. "It does."

"Aren't you eating?"

"I had a sandwich earlier."

His brows rose, and he stared into her eyes.

"Half a sandwich."

He took a deep breath. "You want some of this?"

Her lips turned up into a smile, but she shook her head. "No. I'm not hungry. Thank you, though."

He scooped lasagna on his fork and put it in his mouth. He'd ordered the lasagna two nights ago from Jace at the Sandbar. He didn't really consider himself a cook and only made basic meals here. He ordered from the Sandbar often, and between Jace and Marco, their menu evolved frequently, which kept the boredom down.

He caught Izzy watching him eat. He raised his brows but said nothing. She chuckled again and smiled. "I like watching you eat."

"Good Lord, why?"

She shrugged but said nothing. After scooping the last bite into his mouth, he pushed his plate away and sat back in his seat. Another long swig of his drink finished his meal off perfectly.

He stared at Izzy for a few moments. The sparkle in her eyes, the sass that lay just under the surface, now covered by fear, dimmed her light a bit. But when he'd first walked into the shop the other day, he saw the spunk. Her cheeriness and her happy demeanor. He wanted that back again. He'd figure this out and keep her safe.

"I'm going to take a shower. I can still smell the smoke on me. I'll be out in a few minutes." He pushed himself away, picked up his plate, and set it on the counter, then moved to his bathroom without looking back.

The layout of his condo was simple enough. Open living room, dining room, and kitchen. His bedroom was directly off the living room, a few steps down a short hallway. His bathroom was tucked inside his bedroom. The second bedroom was straight at the end of the short hall. The guest bathroom was directly across from his bedroom. Small, neat, and tidy. He had little to clean and that suited him even better.

Inside his bathroom, he reached into the shower and turned the water on. While the water warmed, he gathered his clothing. Clean boxer briefs, a clean t-shirt, and his sweatpants. He didn't know if Izzy would still be awake when he finished showering, but he hoped so. He meant it earlier when he said he wanted to kiss her again. He'd like to do many things with her, including kissing. Her lips felt wonderful, her body felt perfect against his.

His body began to respond to the direction of his thoughts. He shook his head and stepped into the shower. He groaned slightly after stepping under the warm water. It had been a long day. The warmth of his shower felt good, like a soothing massage over sore muscles. Not that he'd done much today by way of physical activity, but his ribs still hurt, and he wasn't giving them enough rest. He'd rest up after he figured out who wanted to hurt Izzy.

Stepping from the shower, he toweled off, ran his fingers through his wet hair, and dressed. He stepped from the bathroom and froze.

Izzy lay in his bed, on her side, her head propped up on her hand, looking more sensual than any woman he'd ever seen before in his life. Her long blonde hair spilled over her shoulder and shone in the soft light from the lamp at his bedside.

He moved slowly toward the bed in case this was a dream and he'd wake up if he moved too fast. She pulled back the covers for him to slide in beside her, and he was proud he'd done it without a groan. The instant he turned on his right side to face her though, his cock had ideas and he hoped he could help it out with its plan, given his physical condition.

She smiled at him softly, "I wanted to kiss you again, too. And I'd feel safer in here with you."

"I don't know how safe you are in my bed, Izzy."

She chuckled. "I think I'm as safe as I need to be."

He leaned in and kissed her lips. Their kiss became heated quickly, their tongues danced in unison, their lips moved together, and their bodies pressed tightly against each other.

She gently nudged him down on his back and

looked into his eyes. "I don't want you to hurt yourself. Let me do the work."

He chuckled. "You're a dream come true."

She laughed as she straddled him. She wore a loose tank top and lacy panties, and he tucked his forefinger into the waistband and slid it around the top. She grinned before moving off him and shimmying her panties down her sexy legs.

Returning to the bed, she slid her fingers into the waistband of his sweatpants and slid them down. He lifted his ass off the bed to help her out. After pulling them off his legs, her hands slowly moved up his legs, caressing his heated skin. She stopped at the leg of his boxer briefs. Her fingers tucked under the fabric and teased his skin before she slid her hands up his hips and tugged at the waistband of his offending underwear. She tugged them from his body, and this time as her hands explored his legs, she cupped his balls with one hand and wrapped her fingers around his cock with the other.

His breath rushed from his lungs, and all thought went south from there. She pumped him a few times, watching his face as she did. For his part, he didn't know if he wanted to watch her face or her hands as they brought such pleasure to his body.

She pulled away gently, and quickly straddled him once more. This time, her heated skin pressed against his cock. He lifted his hips slightly, and she returned a beguiling smile.

He cleared his throat. "I have condoms in the drawer." He lazily pointed with his finger. She smiled and leaned forward, pressing her delicious breasts against his chest. His hands wrapped around her, kneading her back, pulling her closer to him, enjoying the feel of her weight on him.

She pulled a condom from the drawer and opened the package with deft fingers. She pulled back slightly and slowly rolled the condom over his cock, adding pressure as she did, her fingers grazing his balls sensually.

His breathing came in short bursts as she lifted herself slightly, positioned his cock at her entrance, and, painfully slow, slid down on him.

He groaned out loud, and she let out a soft sigh. He stared into her eyes, green like new summer grass; her lips were full and soft, she was a catch.

She began moving on him, up and down slowly. She was mesmerizing and electric. His body sizzled as she moved on him.

She smiled sweetly, placed her hands on his shoulders gently, and said, "Ready?"

"Yeah."

She lifted and dropped down on him with greater speed. Their skin grew warm and damp; he met her thrust for thrust, his ribs be damned. His hands found her hips, and he held on tightly as she lifted and fell. She was soft and yet firm as her toned thighs rocked his world.

Her breathing became stilted and heavy, soft moans escaped her lips, her body sank lower onto his so her heavy, full breasts lay on his chest. Her movements changed slightly as she ground herself onto his cock. She cried out softly, ending with a long moan as her orgasm rolled through her body. He felt the tightening of her thighs as she came. His orgasm sped quickly forward as his balls tightened painfully, and he felt the first pulse of his orgasm, that beautiful pain and pleasure, shoot from his cock.

He groaned loudly as he pulsed until his orgasm finally stopped. She lay gently on his body, his arms wrapped around hers, holding her close for a while longer. Her head lay on his collarbone, and he pressed his cheek into her hair, inhaling her scent, imprinting this moment in his mind forever. It felt right. This moment felt like nothing he'd ever felt before. He should be scared of that, but he wasn't. He closed his eyes and let that sink in.

The next morning, Mitch stood at the dining room table, a half-drunk cup of coffee cooling beside his laptop. Jayson's encrypted file transfer had come through ten minutes ago. Mitch clicked open the folder and scanned the images, license plate stills, surveillance enhancements, and a partial ID match on the gray SUV's registration.

Travis Landon.

The name made Mitch pause.

Travis was Sadie's boyfriend. And Sadie, Izzy's

close friend, had been in the flower shop, helping with cleanup. If Travis was tied to Noah, and Noah was tied to Delilah, that complicated things fast.

Mitch zoomed in on the enhanced plate shot, confirming it matched the SUV Noah had loaded crates into last night. There was no arguing the timeline. Either Travis was renting out his vehicle, or he was involved.

He picked up his phone and hit Jayson's number.

"Tell me I'm wrong," Mitch said without preamble.

"You're not," Jayson replied grimly. "That SUV is registered to Travis Landon. Pulled from DMV this morning."

"Could it be borrowed? Stolen?"

"Doesn't look like it. No reports filed. And I did a soft pull on Travis, nothing shady on the surface, but I dug through traffic cams. That same SUV was parked outside Sadie's apartment two nights ago. Same plate. Same dents on the fender."

Mitch exhaled through his nose. "So he's not just borrowing it. He's using it."

"Looks that way."

"Was his truck also in Sadie's driveway?"

"Nope. Seems like he must have another place to keep extra vehicles."

"And the guy with Noah last night?"

"Blurry shot, but he fits Travis's general profile. I'm running facial recognition against social media. It'll take time."

Mitch dragged a hand through his hair. This wasn't good. If Travis was involved, it meant whoever orchestrated the fire had someone close to Izzy's inner circle. Someone with proximity. That tightened the noose.

"Pull any cell records yet?" Mitch asked.

"Working on it. But here's the kicker: Travis started receiving regular deposits about three months ago. Small amounts, spaced out. Different accounts. Looks like dirty money being funneled under the radar."

Mitch's jaw clenched. "You think Delilah's bankrolling this?"

"Could be. Or she's a cog in someone else's wheel. Either way, Travis and Noah are both in the mix."

Mitch ended the call and sat back, staring at the wall.

Izzy didn't like Travis. She'd mentioned it. Said something always felt off about the guy. But this? This was a whole different level.

He stood and paced the room. He needed to warn her. But not scare her. Not yet. Not until he had confirmation that Travis was more than just a delivery mule or someone being used. The soft sound of the shower shutting off had his thoughts veering off to a naked Izzy in the other room. It was easy for his thoughts to shift dramatically like that, where she was concerned. Especially after their night together last night. Before, he only wondered and dreamed about what she felt like; now he knew, and it was so much better than the dreams.

The bathroom door opened, and a fresh-faced, smiling Izzy rounded the corner. Her long blonde hair was pulled back into a ponytail at the crown of her head. She wore denim cut-off shorts and a white t-shirt. She was stunning. Tanned legs that went all the way up to her...

"What are you staring at?"

She looked down at her body, then back up to him.

"You." His throat was dry. He took a drink of his coffee. "You look sexy in those shorts."

She chuckled. "Thanks." She grabbed a cup off the counter and poured herself a cup of coffee. Carrying the pot to him, she heated his half-empty cup. He watched her ass as she moved back to the coffee pot. It was a great view.

She turned and saw him staring again, and she laughed. "I can see your thoughts. It's almost like you have thought bubbles above your head."

He shook his head and took a drink of his coffee.

She came to the table, set her cup next to his, and leaned down so they were eye to eye. "You're thinking about last night."

He raised one eyebrow. "I'll think about it all day and maybe tomorrow too."

She stood and picked up her coffee cup. With a wicked grin, she sauntered toward the center island in the kitchen. "Tomorrow you'll be thinking about tonight."

Mic drop. He stared at her, rather dumbfounded

and unable to say a word. When his voice finally reappeared, he cleared his throat and said, "Now I'll be thinking about tonight all day today."

She looked over her shoulder and laughed. "Eggs okay for breakfast?"

"Perfect."

He continued to read Jayson's report and formed his plan for today.

He'd check out Travis's place after he dropped Izzy at the shop. Quietly. Maybe catch a glimpse of the SUV himself or see who came and went.

"Is Sadie coming to help at the shop today?"

"No, she has to work. Ms. Jillie is coming today."

"Who is that?"

"She's a retired lady from town. Her husband died a couple of years ago, around the same time my parents passed. She came into the shop one day and asked if I had anything she could do to help out. She volunteers her time. She comes a couple of days a week. She won't take pay, just says she needs to get out of the house, and she loves flowers. I usually send her home with a bouquet or two each week, and she loves that. Says it brightens her place."

"Okay. That's nice."

It was nice. He was sure Izzy attracted people because of her personality. She was a ray of sunshine.

He texted Jayson.

Start cycling the interior cameras.
Look for any time Sadie came in the
last 48 hours. Watch for Travis, too, if
he ever walked her in.

They finished breakfast and climbed into his truck. As he drove through Blossom Springs, the town looked the same. Quaint. Unassuming. But now every corner hid a shadow. Every smile a potential mask.

Someone close to Izzy was dirty. And Mitch was going to find out who, before they got any closer.

14

Izzy unlocked the front door of Petal Pushers and stepped inside, the scent of fresh greenery and floral preservatives already in the air from the stock she'd prepped yesterday. She inhaled deeply, letting the familiar comfort settle over her shoulders like a warm shawl.

Ms. Jillie was already there, arranging ribbons on a table with surgical precision.

"Morning, sunshine," Ms. Jillie greeted with a warm smile. Her silver hair was swept up in its usual twist, and her cheeks were flushed pink from the early morning hustle.

"Morning," Izzy replied, locking the door behind her. "You beat me again."

Ms. Jillie shrugged. "Old habits. I was awake before the birds, might as well come in and do something useful."

Izzy smiled and moved toward the prep station. "We've got the Saunders funeral this afternoon. Two standing sprays, a casket arrangement, and four vase displays for the tables. They want classic white with greenery. I figured we'd start with the standing sprays?"

"Already started pulling stems," Ms. Jillie said, pointing to a cart loaded with white roses, lilies, hydrangeas, and eucalyptus. "Thought you might like a head start. Looks like you got everything cleaned up yesterday."

"Yes. Sadie came and helped me."

Ms. Jillie smiled. "You've got a good friend in her."

"I do." Izzy pulled on her apron and got to work.

For the next two hours, the shop buzzed with quiet concentration. She and Ms. Jillie worked side by side, trimming stems, soaking foam, and threading in blooms. Conversation was light, mostly about flower techniques and neighborhood gossip. Izzy appreciated the normalcy of it. It made the ugly stuff fade into the distance for a few short hours.

By mid-morning, the last arrangement was secured with ribbon and misted with sealant.

"Would you mind dropping these at Harper's Funeral Home for me?" Izzy asked, rubbing a kink from her neck. "They need everything set up before one."

"Of course." Ms. Jillie patted her shoulder. "You take a breather. I'll be back in half an hour."

Izzy helped her load the delivery van and watched her drive away with a small sense of relief. It felt good to do normal things again. No sabotage, no fear, just flowers and kind company.

She went back inside the shop, locked the door, and pulled the few orders she'd managed to get confirmation on. She checked her inventory to make sure she could handle the orders and relief swept through her. Noah had delivered most everything she'd needed yesterday, with another shipment of flowers coming this afternoon from a different vendor. The back door opened, and Ms. Jillie stepped through the door with a smile on her face. "All delivered and in perfect shape."

"Thank you so much. If we can keep this going, the fire will just be a blip on the radar of all the things here at the shop."

Ms. Jillie nodded. "Let's hope so."

Izzy returned to the cooler and began sorting through flowers for her next arrangement. She was halfway through a container of snapdragons when her phone rang.

"Petal Pushers, this is Izzy."

"Isabelle," came the sharp, annoyed voice of Edgar Harper, the funeral director. "We have a problem."

Her stomach dropped. "What kind of problem?"

"The Saunders family arrangements. The vases are wilted, and the standing sprays look like someone threw them together in the dark. Half the ribbons are missing, and the main casket piece has *carnations* in it."

Izzy blinked. "What? That's not possible. I made the casket piece myself."

"Well, something changed between you making it and it showing up here," Edgar snapped. "This is a funeral, Isabelle, not a middle-school recital. The family is livid. I need it fixed. Now."

"I...I'll be right there." She hung up and stood frozen for a beat.

What the hell?

The arrangements had been perfect when they left the shop. She and Ms. Jillie had double-checked everything. She rushed to the front and grabbed her purse, and texted Mitch.

> Call me. Something's wrong with the funeral flowers. Heading to Harper's now.

Before she left, she hurried to the back. "Ms. Jillie, Edgar Harper just called. He said the flowers are horrible. He said they were wilted and the arrangements were terrible."

"That's just not true. I delivered them myself. They were perfect as always."

"I have to go over there. Please keep the shop open for me."

"Of course, dear."

As she drove, panic twisted in her gut. Who would do this? Who would *touch* a family's funeral flowers and sabotage them?

She arrived at the funeral home and rushed inside. Edgar met her with arms crossed, glaring like she'd vandalized the entire chapel.

"In here," he barked.

Izzy stepped into the viewing room, and her breath hitched. He wasn't exaggerating.

The once-immaculate sprays sagged, several blooms drooping from stems that were clearly no longer water-soaked. The casket arrangement had been dismantled and poorly reconstructed, with carnations hastily jammed between gaps. The vases had visible brown edges on the lilies. One had even been tipped slightly, dripping onto the linen.

Her chest tightened. "This wasn't like this when it left the shop. I swear."

"I don't care where it happened. I care that it's fixed."

Izzy nodded, jaw clenched. "I'll handle it."

She returned to her car and called Mitch, hands trembling.

"Someone tampered with the funeral flowers," she said the moment he picked up. "They were perfect when Ms. Jillie delivered them, and now they look like they've been swapped out or sabotaged. They're wilted and they've been pulled apart and rearranged horribly." Her voice cracked as the tears threatened to spill over. "This was done on purpose to hurt my reputation."

There was a beat of silence before Mitch's voice

came low and serious. "I'll see what kind of cam footage I can find around the funeral home. If someone got to them, we'll find out how." He was silent for only a moment. "Honey, I promise you I'm working to find out who's doing this."

Izzy swallowed. Her heart was pounding, not just from the panic of disappointing a grieving family, but from something worse.

This wasn't random.

This was personal.

15

Mitch gripped his phone tightly, Izzy's distressed voice still ringing in his ears as he stared out the windshield of his truck. His heart ached as he recalled the sound of her voice. So sad. So bewildered why anyone would do this. She hadn't done anything to anyone for all they knew. Not willingly. But these attacks were purposeful and deliberate.

Sabotaging funeral flowers? That was a new low.

He'd been about to pull onto Travis's street when Izzy called. The detour to Harper's Funeral Home wasn't optional anymore. Someone had targeted her again, publicly this time, and they weren't just playing games. They were escalating.

He peeled away from the curb, heart hammering. His mind cataloged possibilities like a checklist: Noah, Travis, Delilah. Was one of them so petty, so calculated, they'd tamper with a grieving family's arrangements just to ruin Izzy's business?

Five minutes later, he pulled into the small parking lot behind the funeral home, parked close to the service entrance, and killed the engine. The place looked quiet. Too quiet. He scanned the exterior, basic security cams over the back door, and the side lot. No visible blind spots. Good.

Inside, he found Edgar Harper pacing in the hallway like a pressure cooker. The older man scowled when he spotted Mitch.

"We're not open for visitation yet."

Mitch took a deep breath. "I'm not here for visitation. I'm here to discuss Izzy Payton and the incident with the flowers."

"If you're here to explain why that girl sabotaged the flowers, save your breath."

Mitch bit back the urge to growl. "She didn't. That's why I'm here. Mind if I take a look at your security system?"

Edgar blinked. "You serious?"

"I don't like people who hurt my friends, Mr. Harper. And I take it personally when someone tries to smear a woman who's done nothing but bring beauty to this town. And frankly, your attitude is unworthy of this situation. Did you bother to try and figure out what happened, or did you just assume, Izzy, a fellow businesswoman, would try to destroy her own reputation?"

Harper's scowl softened slightly. His shoulders lowered, and his mouth hung open for a moment. "Camera's in the office. Follow me."

Mitch followed him into the cramped space and quickly pulled up the external feeds. The time stamp on the delivery lined up with Izzy's estimate. Ms. Jillie appeared on-screen, calm and capable, unloading the arrangements with care. A young staffer from the funeral home helped bring them inside.

No issues. The arrangements looked perfect when Ms. Jillie entered with them, and she wasn't inside long enough to alter them in any way. He saw Ms. Jillie leave a few minutes after bringing in the last arrangement.

Then, a half-hour later, there was movement.

A figure in dark clothing, hood up, back turned toward the camera. Too grainy to make out a face, but they entered through the service door. No hesitation.

"Who's that?" Harper asked, his voice suddenly thin.

"Good question," Mitch muttered. He rewound and slowed the footage. The person carried nothing in and nothing out. Just strolled in like they belonged. And fifteen minutes later, they left the same way. Still empty-handed.

Mitch paused the footage at the best angle and snapped a picture with his phone. The build was wrong for Noah, too slim. Possibly female. But it could've been Travis. He'd need clearer angles to confirm.

"You mind if I forward this clip to my tech guy?" Mitch asked.

Harper nodded. "Just find whoever did this. I've got a grieving family here. Izzy is working on the arrangements, but I don't want this to happen ever again. I have a reputation to uphold."

Mitch turned and stared Harper in the eyes. "So does Izzy."

He felt vindicated a bit when Harper's shoulders slumped.

Back outside, Mitch stepped into the sunlight and dialed Jayson.

"I've got the footage from the funeral home for you."

"Send it," Jayson said.

Mitch fired off the clip. "Someone snuck into Harper's after Ms. Jillie dropped off the flowers and sabotaged them."

"I'll run it through filters. You want me to overlay height estimates?"

"Yeah. And compare movement patterns with Travis and Noah. The build's smaller, but I want to be sure."

"What about Delilah?"

"I'm wondering the same. She's small enough to fit the profile. And it seems she may have a reason."

He hung up, walked the perimeter, and paused by

the service entrance. There was a faint scuff mark near the bottom of the frame. A pry? Maybe. Or just a boot scrape. Hard to tell. He called inside for Harper to join him.

As Harper approached, Mitch pointed to the scuff. "Is this door locked all the time?"

"No, as you saw, Ms. Jillie entered without issue. We leave it open for vendors. We've never had reason to feel as though anyone would come in here and do any damage. It's rather sacred here. If you know what I mean."

Mitch nodded. "Okay." He stood and nodded to Harper. "I suggest, for the time being, you put a note on the door for vendors to call you to be let in."

Harper nodded, turned, and went back inside. Mitch waited until he heard the lock turn before he headed back to the truck. The tension coiled through his body like wire. This wasn't about petty jealousy anymore. Someone was systematically trying to dismantle Izzy's life, her business, her reputation, and her confidence.

And Mitch wasn't going to let it happen.

He started the truck and made a silent vow to find out who did this. Who was doing this to Izzy? Then he'd like to have a real relationship with Ms. Izzy Payton. That is, if she's interested too.

16

After fixing the funeral flowers, Izzy came back to the shop. Her fingers shook as she leaned her hands against the scarred wooden counter she used as a checkout point. Her father had used that counter for years, and she hated to give it up. Plus, it gave the shop that old-fashioned feel. She took a deep breath, pushed away from the counter, and pulled up her orders on her computer. A birthday arrangement for a sixtieth birthday. Reds and silvers. That would be a huge contrast to the all-white funeral flowers. She'd do that one next.

She went to the cooler and pulled out some of the red flowers and set them on the worktable. Ms. Jillie stepped in from the greenhouse carrying a coral arrangement.

"That's pretty, Ms. Jillie."

"Thank you, dear. I did this one for the anniversary

party tonight. I made three of them. I think they turned out lovely."

Izzy smiled and nodded. "That's an understatement."

Ms. Jillie took a deep breath. "Is everything alright at the funeral home?"

"Yes, it's all taken care of."

"I'm really sorry about all of that. I don't know what happened."

"I know Ms. Jillie. It isn't anything you did. Mitch is investigating it right now."

"Oh, he's such a nice man. Handsome too."

Izzy chuckled. "Yes, he's certainly handsome."

Ms. Jillie grinned and took her beautiful arrangement and set it in the cooler to display it to customers.

The bell above the shop door jingled, and Izzy glanced up from her worktable, her fingers still sticky with floral tape. Sadie stepped inside, the sunlight glinting off her sunglasses as she pulled them off and tucked them into the neck of her tank top.

"Hey," Sadie said casually, brushing her hands down the front of her shorts. "Thought I'd stop in, see how things are going."

Izzy forced a smile, trying not to stiffen. "Hey. Thanks for coming by."

Sadie's gaze darted around the shop. "Looks like things are finally back to normal. You and Ms. Jillie handled the funeral arrangements?"

Izzy hesitated, the words catching for half a second

before she nodded. "We did. Although someone tampered with them after delivery."

Sadie blinked. "Wait, what? Are you serious?"

"I wish I wasn't. Someone entered Harper's and ruined them. Wilted flowers, torn ribbons, you name it. I had to remake them all at the funeral home. The wilted flowers had been heated with something, like a heat gun or something."

"Jeez," Sadie muttered. "That's awful."

"It is," Izzy said, the words sharper than she intended. "And it's not the first thing that's happened lately."

Sadie tilted her head. "You think it's the same person behind everything?"

"I don't know," Izzy said carefully. She didn't want to bring Travis into it, not without proof, but she couldn't pretend everything was fine anymore. She took a deep breath and said, "Someone close to me has too much information to even know that I created those funeral arrangements."

Sadie tilted her head. "Do you have any idea who that might be?"

Izzy stopped working and wiped her sticky fingers on the damp cloth sitting on the worktable. "No. There are suspects. Mitch is looking into it."

Sadie's lips pursed together. "You've been quiet around me lately. Is there something I should know?"

Izzy hesitated. "Things have been... off. I'm trying to figure out who might be behind everything."

Sadie's brows furrowed. "What do you mean? Like the fire? The flowers?"

"Yes. And the break-in. The sabotage. It feels personal. Too personal."

Sadie gave a small, nervous laugh. "You think someone has it out for you?"

"I don't know. But it sure seems like it. And I'm just trying to protect myself and the shop."

Sadie folded her arms. "You think it's someone we know?"

"I think it might be someone close enough to know when I'm vulnerable."

Sadie frowned, her eyes narrowing. "Wow. That's... unsettling."

Izzy nodded slowly. "It is."

There was an uncomfortable silence between them.

"Well," Sadie said, shifting her weight, "I hope you figure it out. I can't imagine who'd do something so messed up."

"I hope so too," Izzy murmured, her chest tight. She hated feeling like she couldn't tell Sadie what was going on. But to accuse Travis if it was nothing, was not a good thing for her to do. It would ruin their friendship completely.

Sadie stared at her for a moment, then her lips pressed together. "I've gotta go. Let me know if you need anything."

"I will. Thanks for stopping by."

Izzy watched the door swing shut, Sadie's reaction lingering like static in the air. They hadn't fought, not really, but something between them had cracked. Izzy didn't like keeping secrets, especially from someone who'd been so loyal, but she couldn't tell Sadie everything. Not yet. Not without evidence.

Not without hurting her.

The shop fell quiet again. Izzy glanced at the clock. A little after two. Still hours before closing, but with no customers and her nerves fraying, she decided to clear her head. She finished tidying up the workbench, spritzed the roses in the cooler, and took out the trash bags she'd tied off earlier.

The alley between Petal Pushers and her greenhouse was narrow and mostly empty. She'd always planned to connect them, which would be a space for supplies such as watering cans, nippers, and other tools she used in the shop. Right now, she had the garbage cans near there to fill the space.

The summer sun had shifted behind a cloud bank, casting a gray pall over the brick walls and dumpsters. She hauled two bags to the bins and flipped the lids open.

The soft scrape of a shoe behind her made her pause.

She turned.

A figure stood near the far corner of the building, near the front. Hooded. Dressed in black. Not moving.

Her heart kicked into overdrive. "Can I help you?" she asked, her voice thin but steady.

The figure took one slow step forward, which further shrouded him in darkness.

Izzy backed up a pace, her fingers tightening around the trash bags she still held.

"Stay away from me," she warned.

The voice came low and sharp. "Stop digging."

"What?"

"You keep poking around, you're going to get burned worse than your damn flowers."

Izzy's blood turned to ice.

"I...I don't know who you are, but you need to leave. Right now."

A chuckle, dry and humorless. "No one's coming to save you if you push too far."

She blinked and in that split second, the figure slipped around the corner, disappearing down Main Square.

Izzy stood frozen for several seconds, the only sound was her own harsh breathing. Her hands trembled as she fumbled for her phone and dialed Mitch.

When he picked up, her voice broke. "Someone just threatened me. In the alley between the shop and the greenhouse. I couldn't see their face, but it was a warning, 'stop digging.' Mitch, I'm scared."

"I'm on my way," he said instantly. "Lock the doors. Don't let anyone else in."

She ran inside, heart racing, and twisted the deadbolt into place. She raced to the front of the building and locked the front door too. She braved a look in both directions down Main Square. She saw people coming and going from businesses. No one in a dark hoodie. It was too hot out for that.

This wasn't just about sabotage anymore. It was a full-blown threat.

And whoever was behind it was getting closer.

17

M itch floored the gas pedal, barely slowing for the turn onto Main Square. The second Izzy's voice broke through the phone, frightened and shaking, his entire body had snapped into focus. Every protective instinct surged to the surface like a lit fuse.

She'd been threatened. By someone bold enough to confront her in broad daylight. In her alley.

He spotted the familiar pale green trim of Petal Pushers and pulled into the curb hard enough to jolt the truck. He was out and moving before the engine even quieted. The jolt to his ribs caused him to spit out, "Fuck," but he kept moving.

The front door was locked, but Izzy's face appeared through the window almost instantly. She opened the door with shaking hands, her eyes wide and full of tears that hadn't fallen yet.

Mitch stepped inside and immediately locked the door behind him.

She launched into his arms before he could say a word, clinging to him like she'd been holding herself together by sheer will until now. His arms came around her, strong and steady, one hand cupping the back of her head, the other at her waist. Her shaking body pissed him off. She was so scared that she shook.

"You're safe," he whispered. "I've got you."

Her breath hitched against his chest. "He was just… standing there. Like he was waiting for me."

He leaned back just enough to see her face. "Did he touch you?"

She shook her head quickly. "No. But he said, 'Stop digging or you're going to get burned worse than your flowers.' Mitch, he *knew*. He knew everything."

He swore under his breath and guided her gently to the counter stool, crouching in front of her. "You did exactly the right thing, Izzy. You got out. You called me. And now, I'm going to find out who the hell just threatened you."

She nodded, still trembling, her fingers clenched tightly around his.

"Stay inside," he said firmly. "Don't open the door for anyone except me or Jayson. I'll be right out back looking for evidence."

She sniffed, and his anger grew to a boiling point.

Mitch stepped into the alley, every sense on alert.

His hand hovered near the grip of his concealed weapon, his eyes scanning every shadow. It was a long, clean alley with only the garbage cans partially blocking the back end. He took his phone out and turned on the flashlight. There was a partial boot print in the sandy soil. He snapped a photo of it and looked for a full image. The man had only taken two steps into the alley. No more prints. Mitch turned to look at the businesses across the street. The courthouse stood in the center of Main Square. All other businesses were built around the magnificent courthouse. The post office stood to the left of Izzy's place. To the right was the intersection of Main Square and Main Street. He might be able to get camera footage from the court-house or the post office.

He took a deep breath. The air was thick with late-afternoon heat, but he caught the trace of something else, faint, chemical. Like adhesive or melted plastic.

He moved to the edge of the alley near where Izzy had described the confrontation. A dark scuff marked the brick near the front corner. Nothing unusual by itself, but fresh. Too smudged to be useful, but the direction of the retreat was clear. It looked as though the man turned hastily and scuffed his boot against the wall. That alone wouldn't leave the odor of burnt plas-tic, but with the heaviness of the air, it could have been on his clothing and lingered.

As he followed the route around the corner toward

the post office, past the greenhouse, he saw a partial print on the cement sidewalk from the alley. Thank goodness for heavy moisture on the grass, it showed him the direction the man went. He followed that direction past the greenhouse until he reached the alley between the greenhouse and the post office. It was the alley all the Main Square businesses used to access the backs of their buildings. It traveled both directions behind the post office and Izzy's place. He followed the alley, looking for boot prints that would stop to get into a vehicle. Another print was found on the corner behind the post office. He found no others. He'd have to see about getting footage. A man in a hoodie would've stood out; it was far too hot for that kind of gear.

Mitch took photos of the scuff, the shoe prints, and the alley angle from multiple directions. Then he texted Jayson:

> Possible suspect threatened Izzy. Alley between the shop and greenhouse. Sending pics. Check traffic cams and local feeds. See who left the square between 2:10–2:20 wearing a dark hoodie. Check Izzy's cameras to see where he went.

Back inside, Izzy was pacing. She stopped short when she saw him.

"Nothing concrete," he said, crossing to her. "But I

got some pictures. Jayson's pulling feeds. I'm heading over to the courthouse to see if I can obtain access to their cameras."

Izzy sat down slowly. "He was *right here*, Mitch. He could've... I don't know what he wanted."

"He wanted to scare you," Mitch said, jaw tightening. "And it worked. But that's where it ends."

She looked up, eyes searching his. "What if he tries again?"

"Then I'll be ready." His voice was low, sure. "And next time, he won't get away."

He reached out, brushing a knuckle along her cheek. "You're not alone in this, Izzy. I'm going to stop him, or them, from hurting you."

She closed her eyes and leaned into his touch, exhaling slowly. "Okay."

Mitch glanced out the glass front door toward the street. Business as usual. "You need to close the shop for the rest of today."

"But, I've already lost so..."

"I need to be out and about investigating, and I need to know you're safe. Right now, Sadie isn't an option as long as Travis is a suspect. So, you need to be at my place, where security is abundant."

He watched as she swallowed, took a deep breath, and resigned herself to the truth of his words.

"How will I ever get my business back if I can't be here?"

"I'll help you with that. Once all of this is settled. I've got some amazing friends here, and we'll all help you get Petal Pushers to be the busiest little shop in town. Hell, maybe the state."

She smiled but didn't laugh as he hoped she would. That was his next goal: getting her happiness back.

18

Izzy sat curled in the passenger seat of Mitch's truck, her arms hugging her waist so tightly it felt like the only thing holding her together. Her heartbeat hadn't slowed, not even after Mitch had gotten there and wrapped her in those strong, steady arms. That brief moment of safety was already fading, replaced by the memory of the figure in the alley and the voice that had carved a warning straight into her bones.

Stop digging.

She hadn't even realized how deeply she'd gone. She wasn't an investigator; she arranged flowers. But somehow, she'd stirred up something ugly. Something dangerous.

Mitch's truck rolled to a stop in his driveway, and she barely registered the motion until he shut off the engine and came around to open her door. She slid out like a ghost, numb and silent.

Inside, the familiar scent of him, clean soap, coffee, and a hint of pine, grounded her more than anything else had all day. He locked the door behind them and handed her a glass of water. She took it, her hands trembling so badly some of it sloshed over the rim. He didn't say anything. Just pressed a light touch to the small of her back and guided her to the couch.

"I'm going to do another sweep outside," he said softly. "Won't be long."

She nodded, clutching the glass like a lifeline. As soon as the door clicked shut behind him, the floodgates opened.

Tears spilled over, silent and hot. She pressed the heel of her hand to her mouth to muffle the sound, but it didn't stop the shaking. She hated how scared she felt, how powerless. She hadn't cried when the shop was vandalized. She hadn't cried when the funeral flowers were ruined. But this?

This had been personal. Deliberate. That person had waited for her. Watched her.

She was being hunted, and she didn't even know why.

After a few minutes, she wiped her eyes and stood, needing to move. To *do* something. Her gaze landed on the bag she'd brought from the shop; inside were delivery slips, invoices, anything she thought might help Mitch piece this together. Her fingers skimmed through them absently...until one caught her attention.

It didn't match the others.

The handwriting was uneven. The ink was smeared slightly, like it had been written in a rush. The supplier was *Clearway Supply*, a name she didn't recognize. And it was time-stamped for 11:37 a.m. yesterday.

But no one had come at that time. No deliveries. No drop-offs. No memory of seeing anyone.

Her heart lurched. A chill raced down her spine.

She pulled out her phone with shaking fingers and texted Mitch:

> Do you recognize 'Clearway Supply'? There's a slip for a delivery we never received.

His reply came almost instantly.

> Never heard of it. I'll be right in.

She padded quietly to her bedroom. She changed her clothes. Even though it was in the nineties outside, she was chilled. She pulled on a loose sweater and a pair of jeans. She heard the door open and shut, and jumped behind the door for a moment. She peered around the door frame to see Mitch walking from the living room to the kitchen. She closed her eyes for a moment and took a deep breath. Squaring her shoulders, she stepped from her room and met him at the dining room table.

She handed him the slip wordlessly. He examined it, turning it over in his hand.

He typed into his computer and read his screen before he said anything. "This is a fake," he muttered. "Not only is the supplier unknown, but this isn't your handwriting. And it sure as hell isn't Ms. Jillie's either, is it?"

"No."

His lips turned down for a moment as he stared at the slip. "I'll get this to Jayson. Where did you find it?"

Izzy's mouth went dry. "It was on my desk. Why forge a delivery slip?"

Mitch's jaw clenched. "To create an excuse to be there. Whoever wrote this wanted to appear like they belonged."

"They could've planted something," she whispered. "Or stolen something. Or..." her voice faltered, "I don't know how it got there."

He looked up, their eyes locking. "You didn't find anything else?"

She shook her head. "I'll go through everything I brought again."

"I'll call Jayson right now. We'll look at the security videos and see when this person came into the shop."

She cleared her throat lightly; there seemed to be a clog in it right now. "I thought this was someone being petty. Someone jealous or angry. But this feels like... like we're on someone's radar for a reason I can't see."

"You are," Mitch said quietly. "And I hate that you're in their crosshairs."

Her eyes burned again. "I feel like I'm unraveling. Like no matter how hard I try, someone is always one step ahead. And I'm just waiting for the next hit."

He stepped around the table and pulled her into his arms, this time slower, more deliberate. "You're not alone in this, Izzy. Not anymore. We'll use this, this forged slip, to track them down. Every move they make is going to leave a trail. And we'll follow it."

She closed her eyes and leaned against him, drawing strength from his certainty.

Because she didn't have any left of her own.

But maybe... just maybe... with him beside her, she didn't have to.

19

Mitch sat in front of his laptop, arms crossed, watching the security footage from Petal Pushers for the third time. Jayson was on a video call, his face tense, lit by the blue glow of multiple monitors in front of him.

"There," Jayson said, pausing the feed. "That's your intruder."

The frame showed a figure in a green delivery vest, carrying a clipboard and a box marked *Clearway Supply*. He moved fast, confident, head down to obscure the camera angle.

"Pause it," Mitch said. "Zoom on the box."

Jayson did as asked. The logo was clean, too clean. Not a smudge or a dent on the cardboard. Mitch leaned closer.

"That box is empty," he muttered. "Look at the bottom. No sag. No weight shift. And the angle at which he carries it is a tell. His fingers don't look tight like they would if there was weight in that box."

Jayson nodded. "It's a prop."

"Go back," Mitch said. "I want to see how he got in."

Jayson moved the slider back five minutes in the video. The side alley camera caught the moment the back door clicked open. No break-in. No forced entry.

"He had a key." Mitch's voice went quiet. "Or a copy."

Jayson whistled low. "That narrows the pool."

Mitch's stomach turned. "Ms. Jillie, Izzy, Sadie, Travis..." He trailed off. Ms. Jillie certainly wouldn't do something like this. Sadie wouldn't, at least, he didn't want to believe she would. But Travis?

Jayson kept working. "Want me to cross-reference the footage with the hotel exterior cams?"

"Yeah. He left through the alley. If we're lucky, the hotel caught him heading north. Then cross-reference it with the security cams on the courthouse. We may see which way he heads on Main Square."

While Jayson tapped away, Mitch's eyes drifted to the forged slip resting on the table beside him. His thumb brushed over the edge. Whoever had done this wasn't just playing games; they'd walked into Izzy's sanctuary. Left a fake trace. Threatened her livelihood and her life.

His jaw clenched.

"Got something," Jayson said. "He left the alley,

walked past the post office, then turned into the lot behind Mae's Bakery. Out of view after that, but wait, hold on."

Jayson flipped to a new angle, caught by the camera in the back of Mae's.

"There. Boom. Tan SUV. No plates on the front, but we'll get the rear. Zooming now."

Mitch's pulse quickened. "Can you run it?"

"Already doing it. Give me an hour."

Mitch nodded and leaned back, exhaling slowly.

It was happening. They were closing in. And it was time to get serious.

He turned his head to see Izzy staring at the screen from the kitchen. Her eyes moved to his, and they stared for a moment. He loved looking into her eyes. He'd prefer to do it on a date or while they spent time together, not looking for criminals.

"Did you hear all of that?"

"Yeah."

"We're narrowing it down."

She nodded in reply, her eyes leaving his and staring at the computer screen in front of him. "I know."

Just two words, but they told him everything. She looked into his eyes again. "I trust you. I know you're doing everything you can."

His heart swelled with pride and the newfound trust she'd bestowed on him. To have her trust meant the world to him. He'd work day and night to make sure that trust wasn't misplaced. For the first time in years, he wanted to get to know a woman more. No one had piqued his interest in a long time. But he felt a pull to Izzy, and he wanted to know everything about her. He wanted to have dinner with her and wake up in the morning with her. He liked being in her presence. He liked having her in his space. All of this made him a bit scared and excited all at once. He needed to wrap this up to protect her so she could be in his life in a real way, not as protector and client.

Whoever was behind this had made a mistake.

They came after the wrong woman.

He stood and sauntered to where Izzy stood a few feet away. The instant he was close, she leaned into him and her arms wrapped around his waist. His arms pulled her into his body and held her close. He rested his head on hers, inhaling her sweet scent, enjoying how she felt pulled tightly against him. She felt as if she were made for him. A feeling he'd never felt before rushed through him at the speed of light. A calm came over him as thoughts settled in his mind. She was brought here for him.

Later that evening, after dinner, dishes, and time spent together watching some silly romantic comedy which made Izzy laugh more than him, Mitch stood on his patio, the night thick around him, phone pressed to his ear as he waited for Jayson to answer. The moonlight cast long shadows across the parking lot, but Mitch wasn't watching the trees or the sidewalk. His focus was razor-sharp, his body still riding the electric current of adrenaline that shot through him every time he thought about someone hurting Izzy.

Finally, the line clicked. "Got a hit," Jayson said, his voice clipped and focused. "Ran the rear plate. It's registered to a Samuel Briggs, P.O. Box in Bowling Green. That's a dead-end shell if I've ever seen one."

Mitch swore under his breath. "What about the vehicle?"

"Tan, '09 Trailblazer. No traffic violations, no service records under that tag for the past three years. Either someone's keeping a low profile, or it's a burner."

"Anyone local tied to it?"

"Working on it, but here's the thing," Jayson said. "I pulled old footage from around Petal Pushers the day of the fire. The same SUV was parked across from the alley. Just sitting there for about twenty minutes. Engine running. Someone was watching her even then."

Mitch's hand curled into a fist. "Is it possible to get hotel camera footage for the alley for the thirty days prior to the first break-in? I'd like to see how long this asshole has been stalking her. Watching her patterns. And if he has ties to Delilah or anyone else we're suspicious of."

"I'll see what I can do on that front. So far, the Hotel has been great to work with. They don't like the idea of someone out there hurting Izzy or anyone else." Jayson said.

Mitch's blood turned cold.

He hung up and walked back inside. Securing the locks on the door and pushing the stop down to ensure no one entered. He paused to look at Izzy asleep on the couch. She'd dozed off under a throw blanket, her face soft in the low light, the crease between her brows finally relaxed. Seeing her like that, safe, for now, burned into him. It made everything else background noise.

He wasn't sure when this had changed from a mission to a personal matter, but it was that now and so much more.

He crossed the room quietly, sat in the armchair across from her, and opened his laptop. He reviewed every note he and Jayson had compiled. Every time stamp. Every event. The explosion. The fake delivery. The floral sabotage. The threat in the alley. Someone was getting closer and bolder. They now entered the building.

Whoever it was knew her schedule, her habits, even how to manipulate the people around her. And they weren't finished.

His eyes landed on the digital image of the Clearway Supply slip again.

The handwriting was messy. Not panicked. Just rushed.

He leaned in closer. Something about the slant of

the letters tugged at a memory. He'd seen handwriting like that on something. He closed his eyes for a moment trying to drag the memory from the depths of his mind. Ah, finally, he recalled. It was a witness statement.

He opened his archived files, cross-referenced the loops in the capital letters. The slant of the lowercase 't.' The angular hook on the 'y.'

Then it hit him like a gut punch.

The handwriting matched an old report from Travis Fielder's past, back when he'd been caught forging documents at his father's garage to pocket extra cash. The charges had been dropped, but Mitch had remembered it because Travis had been arrogant and smug, even under pressure.

And the writing? It was now burned into Mitch's brain.

He copied both images and texted Jayson:

> Pull Travis's employment records. I think we've got a match.

Then he stood, quietly turning off the lamp. He walked to the couch and gently shifted Izzy's blanket so it covered her better. Her lashes fluttered, but she didn't wake. He lingered for a long second, hand hovering near her cheek but not quite touching.

She was the strongest person he knew, and still, someone had tried to break her.

He wouldn't let it happen.

Izzy stirred to the soft hum of the refrigerator and the faint smell of coffee drifting from the kitchen. For a long moment, she didn't open her eyes. The throw blanket was warm against her skin, and the quiet safety of Mitch's living room wrapped around her like a cocoon.

Last night's terror still lingered at the edge of her mind, the voice in the alley, the forged slip, but so did the memory of Mitch's arms around her, the way he'd held her like she wasn't just someone to protect but someone he cared about.

She exhaled slowly and sat up, adjusting the blanket around her shoulders. Her fingers brushed the couch cushion where Mitch had tucked it beneath her head. She hadn't meant to fall asleep. But she must have felt safe enough to let go. That thought made her smile.

A quiet clink came from the kitchen. She stood and padded toward the sound.

Mitch stood at the stove, barefoot, hair a tousled mess, his T-shirt stretched tight across his shoulders. His muscles bunched and stretched as he stirred something in a pan. He looked over his shoulder when he heard her.

"Morning," he said, voice low and warm. "I didn't want to wake you."

"You didn't." Her voice came out husky. "I feel like I slept for the first time in days."

He nodded toward the counter. "Coffee's fresh. I'm scrambling eggs."

She poured a cup and wrapped both hands around the mug, letting the warmth seep into her palms. "Thanks. For everything. For... last night. For letting me crash here. For keeping me safe."

"You don't have to thank me, Izzy." He met her gaze. "I want you safe. Always."

A flutter caught in her chest. She looked down quickly, trying to get her thoughts in order. "I was thinking this morning... about when things actually began to happen at the shop. I'd wake at night thinking I heard someone downstairs. When I got up and listened at the door, I wouldn't hear anything, and I told myself I had an active imagination. Then one day, I couldn't find my pruning shears. I always hang my garden tools up on the pegboard in the back of the greenhouse. Always. I despise searching for things; it's a waste of time."

Mitch straightened his shoulders. "When did these things begin happening?"

"I think about three weeks ago."

"Did anything happen just before then that could have prompted this? Did someone get upset with you? Did anyone ask something of you and you turned him or her down? Did someone offer to buy the shop? Anything small could mean something."

Izzy stared at the counter for a few moments, then inhaled deeply and looked up at him. "I remembered something weird from a couple of weeks ago," she continued. "Travis was in the shop helping me after that pipe burst in the greenhouse. He was going through my key drawer to grab the water shutoff key, and I remember him saying something about how I should organize them better. That was about two or three weeks ago, but now..."

Her stomach twisted. "What if he made a copy then?"

Mitch turned to face her fully, his expression unreadable. "You're sure you had the entry key in that drawer?"

She nodded. "Positive. I carry one on my keyring, but I had an extra one in the drawer in case I needed to temporarily give someone a copy. Like a repairman or seasonal help."

He turned and set the spatula down, then moved toward her. "That helps. A lot. Jayson's running a few things today. Between that and the footage, we're going to get answers."

Izzy set the mug down before her trembling hands betrayed her. "This was never supposed to happen. I wanted a quiet life. Flowers and peace and people I care about."

"You still get to have that," Mitch said softly. "We just have to take care of this first."

She looked up at him. His eyes were steady, grounding. "You've done more than I ever expected. More than anyone's ever done for me."

He stepped closer. "It's not about duty anymore, Izzy. It hasn't been for a while."

The breath caught in her throat. The silence between them was filled with something heavy, electric. She felt it too, but was afraid to say it out loud in case she scared him away.

"I don't know what's happening between us," she whispered. "But I'm scared of losing it before I even understand it."

"You won't lose me," Mitch said. "Not now. Not when we're just getting started."

She swallowed hard, emotion welling up behind her ribs; it was almost hard to take a breath. "Good. Because I'm not sure I could take one more loss."

He reached out and brushed a knuckle along her cheek. "Then we won't let that happen."

The moment stretched between them. A promise. A fragile hope.

And beneath it, the truth: they were getting closer. To each other. To whoever had done this.

And to finally put an end to the fear.

21

Mitch paced the length of the living room, his phone pressed tightly to his ear, as Jayson's voice filtered through the line.

"I ran that Trailblazer again," Jayson said. "Found another sighting, this time parked near Delilah's salon three days ago."

Mitch stopped short. "Delilah's place?"

"Yeah. Could be a coincidence, but I doubt it."

A cold knot formed in Mitch's gut. "Send me the clip."

"It's already on your laptop. And here's the kicker: remember the fake delivery footage? I looped in facial recognition software with the hoodie guy, just for grins. Even with the hoodie and the cap, we got a partial match."

Mitch's breath stilled. "You're kidding."

"Ninety-two percent probability," Jayson said. "It's Travis Fielder."

Mitch let out a long breath through his nose, pressure building at his temples. "Son of a bitch."

"I'm still cross-referencing it with DMV photos and old school yearbooks. But here's something else, I blew up the footage and noticed something tucked in his back pocket."

Mitch dropped into his chair at the dining room table and opened the new file. The still frame showed the man walking away from the shop in the green vest. A smudge of white paper peeked from the back pocket. Jayson had zoomed in and circled it in red.

"That's a folded delivery slip," Mitch said under his breath.

"Right," Jayson replied. "Which begs the question, why carry the forged invoice *out* of the shop? Or did he steal one to make it look like Izzy was incompetent?"

"Because it was always a prop," Mitch said slowly. "A piece of misdirection. He wanted someone to see it. On camera. He wanted to *look* like a real delivery driver. So if we traced it later, it would throw us off."

"Ballsy," Jayson said. "And dumb. But Izzy found a delivery slip on her desk."

"Yeah. So then I'm wondering if he stole one."

Mitch stared at the frozen frame, anger burning low in his gut. "He's overconfident. Arrogant. He thinks he's untouchable."

"He also knew there were cameras, Mitch," Jayson

added. "I'd bet Sadie told him. Or he saw us installing them."

Mitch leaned back, piecing it together. "So, he walks in with a fake delivery, hoping that if someone checks the tapes, they see a 'random supplier.' Meanwhile, he's probably planting something. Bugging the shop. Or just scoping out how far he can push."

"He's getting bold," Jayson agreed. "And we've got enough now to start putting pressure on him."

Mitch nodded, his jaw tightening. "Don't tip our hand yet. Let me dig into his background a little more. See if there's something we missed."

"You got it," Jayson said. "Call me when you're ready."

Mitch ended the call and stared at the paused image on his screen. Travis had made a critical mistake, not just forging a slip, and not just walking into the shop pretending to belong.

He'd underestimated Mitch.

He stood and looked toward the hall as the bathroom door opened. Izzy sauntered around the corner looking fresh as a daisy. Her long blonde hair was pulled back into a ponytail at the crown of her head. Her face was soft, and her eyes were clear. She said she'd slept well last night, it showed.

She trusted him so much that she was able to put aside all this turmoil and get some sleep.

Now it was time to prove that trust was well-placed and finish this.

Mitch pushed back from the table, his thoughts racing faster than his pulse. Every time he peeled back a layer, Travis looked guiltier. And now that the footage lined up, the Trailblazer sightings, the forged slip, it was becoming undeniable.

But he still didn't have enough to take to the sheriff. Not yet. This needed to be airtight. No room for reasonable doubt. Because if Travis caught wind that they were onto him, he'd vanish. Or worse, he'd escalate.

He grabbed a notepad and started listing what they had:

- SUV sighting at Delilah's
- Hoodie footage match: 92% confidence
- Forged delivery slip, possibly a stolen delivery slip
- Key access likely traced to Izzy's spare
- Video of back entrance entry, no forced access
- Pattern of sabotage escalating over weeks

Then he started a second column:

Next steps

- Pull Travis's employment history
- Compare handwriting sample from past case
- Interview Ms. Jillie quietly
- Look for digital footprints, any online activity?
- Determine if Delilah knows more than she's letting on

He tapped the pen against the table. Delilah. Her name stuck in his mind like a sliver. If Travis had parked near her salon recently, and if Sadie had been at work during that shift, there was a chance Travis had so much more going on than Sadie was aware of.

Izzy walked toward the kitchen, barefoot and quiet, reaching for her coffee cup. Mitch crossed over and lightly touched her elbow.

"Hey," he said, voice low. "You okay?"

She nodded. "Yeah. I feel better now that I actually slept."

He gave her a soft smile. "I noticed."

She tilted her head. "What are you working on?"

"Trying to stitch this all together." He motioned toward the table. "Travis is connected. I'm sure of it. We've got surveillance, the SUV, even a partial facial match. But I need one more thing to make it stick."

Her eyes darkened. "I want to help."

He hesitated, then gave a slight nod. "Actually... I could use your memory. Think back. Has anyone else come in asking strange questions? Anyone new around the shop the last few weeks, delivery people, maybe someone just browsing?"

Izzy leaned against the counter, thinking. "Besides the fake Clearway guy? Not that I can recall. Most of our customers are locals or regulars." Her brows pinched together, "Except..."

She swallowed. "There was a guy who came in about three weeks ago asking if we do large event arrangements. Like for fundraisers or political dinners. But when I asked what date he needed them for, he didn't have an answer. Just said he was 'gathering quotes.' I remember thinking he didn't look like someone planning a fundraiser."

"What'd he look like?" Mitch asked sharply.

"Older. Mid-forties maybe. Taller than you. Wore a ball cap and sunglasses, inside. He kept his voice low, like he didn't want to be overheard."

Mitch's protective instincts flared. "You didn't tell me about this."

"I didn't think it was anything. He left after a minute or two. Didn't even take a brochure."

Mitch scribbled another note. "That could've been Travis sending someone to scout. Or it was him in disguise. He's bold enough."

She nodded, her mouth pressing into a thin line. "What do we do next?"

He took a steadying breath. "We close this loop. Quietly. I'll stop by the library and talk to Sadie. Discreetly. I need to know if Travis said anything about the cameras or the keys to her."

"That will tip her off."

"It might. Depending on her reaction, we'll confront Travis before he knows he's cornered."

Izzy's shoulders stiffened. "Be careful."

He reached for her hand and gave it a gentle squeeze. "I will. I'm not taking any more chances."

As she looked up at him, something unspoken passed between them, an understanding deeper than words. He could see it in her eyes. The fear was still there, yes, but so was the fight.

"Thank you."

He kissed her lips lightly and pulled her in for a hug. "I think you should stay here today and not go into Petal Pushers."

"I can't do that." She pulled away and looked up at him. "Customers are already slow to come back after the fire. I haven't done any advertising because I don't have my inventory where it needs to be, so only a few brave folks are coming in. I can't lose the few customers I have by not being open. Consistency, I need consistency."

"You need to be safe."

"Ms. Jillie will be in today."

He took a deep breath and squeezed her tightly. "I don't like it, but I admire you, Iz."

She wasn't running.

And neither was he.

22

The moment Izzy stepped into Petal Pushers, the scent of lavender and fresh greenery wrapped around her like an old friend. But the comfort she usually felt here didn't settle in. Not today.

The air was heavier now. Tense. As if the walls themselves remembered what had been done. The faint smell of smoke lingered. In a bar-b-que restaurant, the smell of wood fire was enticing. Here, it was a reminder of something sinister.

She paused at the doorway, letting the stillness settle before stepping inside. Ms. Jillie had already opened up and was at the counter unpacking a box of vases. The older woman glanced up and gave a warm smile, but Izzy could still see the faint worry behind her eyes.

"Morning, sweetheart," Ms. Jillie said. "I was just

restocking the display shelves. Didn't want to mess with anything special."

Izzy nodded and walked behind the counter. "Thanks, Ms. Jillie. I'm going to check the greenhouse and water the plants."

Ms. Jillie reached over and gently squeezed her hand. "You take your time."

The greenhouse behind the shop still carried that faint, damp smell from last week's pipe issue and, again, the smoke. Sunlight spilled in through the high windows, dancing over rows of potted begonias and peace lilies. Izzy walked slowly, scanning everything.

She wanted to believe this was still hers. Her place. Her peace. But paranoia slid in around the edges like a creeping fog.

When she reached the pegboard, her breath hitched.

The pruning shears were gone. Again.

Her pulse quickened. She stepped closer, checking the pegs. No note. No tag moved. No tools shifted.

Just... missing.

She turned slowly, taking in every detail of the space. One of the floor mats by the service sink was slightly askew. She hadn't noticed that before. Had someone come back here? After she closed up for the day yesterday?

Her throat tightened. She hurried to the front of the store. "Ms. Jillie, did you go into the greenhouse this morning?"

"No dear, I came in and saw the boxes stacked from yesterday's delivery, and began unpacking them. Why, is something wrong?"

"I don't know. I hope not."

She pulled out her phone and texted Mitch.

Shears missing again. Greenhouse floor mat looks moved.

His reply came a moment later.

On my way. Don't touch anything.

She pocketed her phone and backed up a few steps, her heart thudding. Looking up, she saw Ms. Jillie watching her, her brows wrinkled in concern. Izzy tried to smile, but it felt as fake as it likely looked.

"Izzy?"

She shook her head. This sweet little lady would think she was going mad if she started blathering on about missing shears and a mat that was crooked. Big deal.

"I'm okay. I just seem to have misplaced my pruning shears."

Why? Why take the shears? They weren't valuable. They weren't even new. But the message was clear: *I was here. I can still get in.*

Her fingers curled into fists. She wouldn't let fear take root. Not here. Not anymore.

By the time Mitch arrived, she'd moved back into the shop, pacing near the front window.

"You okay?" he asked, stepping in with that focused intensity she was beginning to crave. She nodded, swallowing the tight lump in her throat.

"In the greenhouse," she said quietly.

He didn't hesitate. He disappeared into the back, and she followed at a distance. Mitch crouched by the mat, then stood, scanning the area with sharp eyes.

"Definitely disturbed," he muttered. "And you're sure the shears were there yesterday?"

"Yes," she whispered. "They were right there." She pointed at the empty hook.

Mitch turned toward her, his expression grim. "He came back."

He didn't need to say the name. They both felt it.

"I thought maybe we were getting close to the end of this," she said, her voice trembling. "But now it just feels like he's reminding us that we're not done yet."

Mitch closed the distance between them and took her hands. "We are getting close. This is him lashing out, making noise before he's caught. He must enjoy scaring you."

She met his eyes, holding onto them like they were a lifeline. "Do you ever wonder what I did to deserve this?"

"You didn't do anything wrong," he said firmly. "This isn't about you being a target. It's about him being a coward. A manipulator. And we're closing in."

His words soothed something raw inside her. But it was more than reassurance, it was the way he said *we*. Like she wasn't alone in this fight. Like maybe, just maybe, she had someone willing to face the storm with her.

He lifted one hand to her cheek, letting it rest there for a beat. "I meant what I said, Izzy. I'm not going anywhere."

She leaned into his touch, her voice barely a whisper. "I believe you."

They stood like that for a long moment, until the buzz of Mitch's phone broke the spell.

He glanced at it. "It's Jayson. He might have something. I had him check the cameras."

Izzy nodded. "Go. I'll begin watering the plants." She stepped away a couple of steps, then stopped.

"I'll have Jayson here in a few minutes to change the locks."

"I can call a locksmith."

He hesitated, then leaned in and brushed a kiss to her temple. "Not until we know who we can trust. We'll keep this in-house right now. Go to the drawer and pull all the keys to any of the outside doors. I'll take this call."

She nodded and turned toward the shop. After stepping into her office, she opened the top drawer of her desk and pulled out the keys from inside. She took a deep breath. Travis was correct; she should have had them secured and organized. She'd do that from now on.

She spent time sorting the keys. There were two keys to the front and back doors. And two keys to the fertilizer shed out back. One key to the cash register and one to the safe.

Her brows shot up into her bangs. She inserted the key into the safe and opened the door. Inside, she had a zippered bank bag where she kept cash, checks, and receipts. That was there. She pulled it out and opened it. Yesterday's money, complete with deposit slip for today, lay neatly inside.

She had a safe deposit key at the bottom of the bag and an extra key to her delivery van.

The only other things in the safe were her mother's wedding and engagement rings. The blue velvet box still lay at the back of the safe. She pulled the box out and opened the top. Her mother's rings glinted and sparkled in the overhead light. She remembered her mom wearing the rings every day. But she insisted Izzy take them upon her death, and if you don't honor your loved one's wishes after they're gone, what kind of person are you?

Mitch crouched by the back door of Petal Pushers, his tools spread out on the concrete, while Jayson held the flashlight steady overhead. The late morning sun filtered through the alley, but it wasn't enough light for installing locks.

"Old locks are trash," Jayson muttered, rattling one loose in his free hand. "Anyone with a bump key could get in."

"Or someone who had a real key," Mitch said tightly.

Jayson gave him a sidelong glance but said nothing. They didn't need to say Travis's name again. It hung heavy in the air, just like the tension between the bricks.

Mitch slid the new deadbolt into place and tightened the screws. He moved on to the doorknob, hands practiced but mind spinning. He kept seeing the empty hook in the greenhouse. The skewed mat. Izzy's pale face when she'd whispered, *"He came back."*

Damn it. He should've anticipated another move. That's what pissed him off most, being one step behind. He prided himself on always being ahead of threats. But this time, the enemy knew the layout, the schedule, the weaknesses.

"You okay?" Jayson asked, brow raised.

"Not until this guy's in cuffs," Mitch replied, voice sharp.

Jayson nodded. "Fair. But we're close. Too many coincidences stacked together. We just need a little more to push it over the edge. A confirmation of who it actually is. His face as he enters."

Mitch finished the back lock and stood, rubbing his palm across the back of his neck. "Did you hear anything back on Travis's work history?"

Jayson tapped his phone. "Yeah. Spotty employment. Mostly under-the-table stuff. He worked at his cousin's auto shop for a few months after high school but left after a disagreement. Couple of cash gigs, construction, odd jobs. But nothing steady in the last year. Guess where he was fired from a few months ago?"

Mitch's jaw tightened. "No clue."

"He worked as night security at a warehouse in Summerville."

Mitch nodded. "That's why he decided to freelance as a security agent."

"Bingo."

Mitch blew out a breath, gears turning. "Why'd he get fired?"

"According to the notes HR kept, he missed shifts, got confrontational, then would show up at odd hours when he wasn't scheduled."

"Doing what?"

Jayson shrugged. "No notes on that."

"And Sadie never mentioned anything about Travis' spotty work history to Izzy."

"Maybe Sadie doesn't even know. He started his own company. Sadie could think he's entrepreneurial."

Mitch shook his head. "True. Or she might know more and is embarrassed."

Jayson shrugged. "Everybody's hiding something."

Mitch reached for the new lockset for the front door, frustration humming beneath his skin. "Let's get this done."

They worked in silence for a few minutes. Then Jayson said, "You know, he was seen by that courthouse camera again, last night. Just standing across the street from the shop. Not doing anything. Just watching."

Mitch's blood turned to ice. "Stalking her in plain sight."

"Yeah," Jayson said. "Like he's daring us to catch him."

Mitch's grip tightened on the screwdriver. He

finished the install, then stood and faced Jayson. "We lay the trap. We stop waiting for him to strike. We get ahead of him."

"You thinking bait?"

"Something like that," Mitch said. His gaze shifted toward the shop counter where Izzy worked with Ms. Jillie, arranging flowers. She turned her head as if she could feel him watching her and offered a small smile.

It settled something in him. She smiled. Her trust. It made him feel whole.

"This ends soon. One way or another." Mitch quietly said to Jayson.

Mitch and Jayson moved their tools and locks to the front door. Mitch crouched down and began removing the door handle and lock from the old wooden door. He began working on the lock as Jayson removed the strike plate and pulled the new locks from the package. The clink of metal tools echoed in the quiet shop as Ms. Jillie hummed faintly in the background, arranging lilies and hydrangeas at the display table. Izzy worked on red roses in a vase. When she handled the flowers, she looked peaceful and happy. This was her happy place. At least it used to be.

"She's lucky you caught this," Jayson said under his breath. He looked closely at the old lock in his hand. "The frame was scored. Someone's used that lock a lot, or picked it." He held it out to Mitch.

Mitch examined the damaged lock, running the pad of his thumb gently over the scratches on it. "Yeah.

And they're getting bold. Watching from across the street, creeping around the greenhouse. This guy thinks he owns the place." He pulled his thumb away and showed it to Jayson. Small shards of golden metal gleamed on his thumb. "This is fresh."

Someone approached the front door, and a chipper voice called out, "Morning!"

Mitch stiffened. He looked over his shoulder just as Noah stepped in, balancing a cardboard box in one arm and flashing an overly friendly grin.

"Got a surprise delivery," Noah said. "Said it was urgent, fresh orchids from McHenry's. They didn't say why it didn't come in with yesterday's batch."

Mitch stepped back as Noah entered the shop. Izzy smiled, though it didn't reach her eyes. She met Noah at the wooden checkout counter near the middle of the room. "Thank you. That's strange, I didn't order these."

Noah chuckled, scratching the back of his neck. "You didn't?"

"No."

Noah handed her a slip of paper and noticed Izzy's fingers shaking as she took it. He watched as she read the paper, and he saw her swallow. Mitch stepped closer.

"You didn't order these?"

"No. The invoice says I did. But I didn't. Orchids need attention. And I don't have any orders to fill with these."

Noah shrugged. "I don't know what to say. They asked me to deliver them."

Izzy swallowed again but said, "Okay. Do you mind putting them in the cooler?"

Noah shook his head, "Not at all."

Noah carried the container to the cooler. Izzy stared into his eyes for a moment. She shook her head, "I didn't order them." Her brows bunched, and she looked at Ms. Jillie, "Did you order them, Ms. Jillie?"

"No, honey. I only order when you ask me to."

Noah returned from the cooler and set Izzy's pruning shears on the countertop. "You left your favorite pair of pruners in the cooler, Izzy."

Izzy stared at the shears as if they were poison. She absently whispered, "Thanks."

"No problem. You were probably looking for them."

Izzy nodded. "Yes. Thank you. I was."

Noah nodded. "Glad I found them then."

Noah stared at Izzy, and Mitch's jaw tightened. Noah then turned to Mitch. "I didn't mean to interrupt anything."

"You didn't." Mitch rattled the old lock in his hand. "We're just changing out locks. Shop's had some trouble lately."

Noah's gaze lingered on the old hardware. "Yeah? That's gotta be rough. Izzy doesn't deserve that." He looked over at her. "You doing okay?"

Izzy offered a polite smile. "Thanks, Noah. I'm fine."

"You sure? If there's anything I can do, anything at all..."

"She's good," Mitch interrupted. "But thanks."

Jayson moved past them and began packing up the old locks. Mitch held Noah's gaze until the man gave a nervous half-shrug and backed toward the door.

"Alright, well... see you around."

Once Noah left, Mitch turned to Jayson. "That didn't feel right."

"Nope. Creepy vibe's off the charts."

"He knows now that the locks are being changed. That may escalate his behavior, if he's our guy."

Izzy stepped toward them. "I thought you were looking at Travis."

Mitch turned to look into her eyes. "Honey, we're looking at everyone."

Izzy's shoulders slumped. "Oh my Lord. I don't even know what to think or do. I feel like everything about this place is jinxed."

Mitch faced her and placed a hand on each of her shoulders. He bent his knees to look into her eyes. "It isn't jinxed, but someone wants you scared. Maybe scared enough to sell the shop."

She inhaled a deep breath and nodded slowly. "Who wants me gone except Delilah?"

Mitch shook his head. "Maybe just Delilah, and she enlisted help."

Izzy's green eyes stared into his for a long time. He grinned. "We're changing our tactics. Setting a trap to finally get ahead of whoever it is. Now, answer a quick question for me. Have you even taken your pruning shears into the cooler?"

She shook her head slowly. "No. Those are only kept in the greenhouse."

Mitch nodded, then looked at Jayson.

Jayson smirked. "I'm on it."

Later that night, Mitch sat at the dining room table, his laptop open in front of him. Footage from the courthouse camera played on a loop, grainy night video of Noah's car parked along the curb across from Petal Pushers. Just sitting. Lights off. Engine cold.

"Three nights this week," Jayson said, from the computer screen, pointing at the timestamps. "Not delivering. Not moving. Just watching."

Mitch's jaw clenched. "Why the hell is he watching her shop at 11 p.m.?"

Jayson responded. "And Noah leaves, then about fifteen minutes later, it looks like Travis appears on the sidewalk and watches the shop."

The quiet of the condo felt heavier tonight. The faint hum of the refrigerator and the occasional creak of settling walls were the only sounds. Izzy curled up on the couch, a blanket pulled over her legs. Despite the oppressive heat outside, she felt chilled, and a cooling cup of chamomile tea rested on the side table. Her phone sat in her palm, thumb hovering over a name she hadn't called in days.

Their last conversation had ended with tension and an ache that hadn't quite faded. But everything that had happened since the break-in, the missing shears, the surprise orchids, had frayed Izzy's nerves to the point where staying silent felt worse than the risk of reaching out. They usually talked every day, unless they were super busy, but never went more than a day in between at a minimum, chatting on the phone.

She tapped the call button.

Sadie picked up on the second ring. "Hello?"

"Hey," Izzy said softly.

There was a beat of silence. Then, "Hey."

Izzy hesitated, her heartbeat sped up, then she pushed forward. "I wasn't sure if I should call."

"Me, either," Sadie admitted. Her voice sounded tired, guarded.

"How are you?"

"Busy," she replied. "Travis has been... well, he's not around much lately. Always out late. Says it's work."

Izzy bit her lip. "He's still doing the security stuff?"

"Yeah. Sort of." She sighed heavily. " I don't know. He's vague. Says he's meeting with clients, but when I ask who or where, he gets defensive. Tells me to stay out of his business."

Izzy took a breath. "I changed the locks at the shop today."

Sadie's tone sharpened. "Something happen?"

"Yeah. Someone was back inside. Took my pruning shears again. Moved things around. And there was a surprise delivery I didn't order."

Sadie was quiet for a moment. "God, Izzy. That's awful. Are you okay?"

"I'm rattled. But Mitch and Jayson are on it. Mitch thinks we're getting close."

"Do you know who it is?" Sadie asked, her voice barely above a whisper.

Izzy hesitated. "We have suspicions, but nothing concrete."

"I've been thinking about this a lot. I've been wondering if it was Travis," Sadie admitted. "He comes home smelling like smoke sometimes. Not like cigarettes, like... something chemical. And he's so tense. Distant. And the nights you've had issues, he's been out. And, Izzy, I keep wondering if there's someone else in his life."

Izzy closed her eyes. "Sadie..." She swallowed, not sure how much she should say. But this was her best friend. She wouldn't do anything to hurt her. She took a deep breath and rushed on. "Has he ever mentioned Delilah?"

"Delilah Parker?"

"Yes."

Another pause. "He said once she wanted his help securing her salon. But lately...I don't know, he hasn't said anything about her or any of his clients. He gets texts he won't show me. Leaves the room to take calls. He used to leave his phone lying on the counter or coffee table all the time, but now he holds on to it like he'll die without it." She sniffed. "But Delilah?"

Izzy closed her eyes. "We've seen him on camera going into her salon from the back door. More than once and sometimes at night."

The silence dragged on so long she worried Sadie had hung up. "Fucker."

"You don't deserve that. And admittedly, I don't know what they are doing. It could be work-related."

Sadie gave a broken laugh. "I keep telling myself he's just stressed. But I feel like I'm going crazy trying to justify his behavior. And now I'm going to do a little sleuthing on my own."

"You're not crazy. But you sure do need to be careful."

"I'll be careful. I've heard rumors about him being a bad boy. I thought they were jealous."

"Who told you he was a bad boy?"

"Different people who've come into the library. Mostly some of the girls we went to high school with, and some of the guys, too. I thought they were just raining on my parade."

Izzy kept her voice soft. "I never wanted you to be hurt. I'm sorry I have to be the one to tell you this, and honestly, I hope I'm wrong. I miss you."

Sadie was silent for a long moment. Then, quietly, "I miss you too."

They sat in that shared silence, the fragile bridge between them finally starting to rebuild.

Sadie broke it first. "Be careful, Iz. I don't know what's going on, but it feels ugly."

"I will. And Sadie... if you ever need anything. Or need out to get out, you know where to find me."

"I know. Thanks."

They said goodbye, and the call ended, but the weight in Izzy's chest didn't lift. Not yet.

Still, for the first time in days, it didn't feel like she was facing the storm alone.

25

M itch stood in the alley behind Petal Pushers, the hotel, the gas station, Miracle Garage, and Delilah Parker's nail salon. He was near the hotel, where he could hide himself near shrubs and foliage if need be, his arms crossed as he watched the back of Delilah's. The "Closed" sign hung in the front window despite it being mid-morning when he'd driven by earlier. He'd been standing in the alley for twenty minutes now, leaning against a lamppost with a paper coffee cup in hand, playing the part of an average hotel guest enjoying the morning sun.

Except he wasn't. He was hunting.

Jayson's voice buzzed in his ear through the wireless comm link. "Confirmed. Travis was seen on the alley cam again. Last Thursday, midnight. Entering through the back of Delilah's. No delivery bag. No tool-box. Just him, slipping inside like he owned the place."

Mitch ground his jaw. "That's the third time we've caught that."

"Fourth," Jayson corrected. "He was also seen Monday night. Same deal."

"Hmm," Mitch muttered. He took a sip of the now-cold coffee, more out of habit than need. "She doesn't have appointments that late. So what's worth sneaking in for?"

"Cash?" Jayson offered. "Or drugs. We've got a solid lead suggesting Travis is dealing. Maybe she's letting him use the salon to stash or move product."

"Or she's in on it," Mitch said darkly.

"She's certainly not discouraging him."

Mitch's mind turned over the implications. Delilah had debts, two delinquent loans that should've disqualified her from any business expansion. Yet somehow, this morning, lumber had been delivered, and rumor had it, her salon was being remodeled, her supply orders had doubled, and her Instagram account was full of flashy "Coming Soon" posts.

"Travis might be funding her with the drug money," Mitch said aloud. "But that doesn't explain the sabotage at Petal Pushers. Unless Delilah wants Izzy gone so her salon can expand into the flower shop's space."

"Or she's just vindictive," Jayson added. "We've both seen smaller motives spark bigger crimes."

Before Mitch could reply, the salon's back door

creaked open. He stepped behind the post and angled himself just enough to watch. Delilah emerged in platform heels and a sleek, gold-trimmed dress that didn't say "business owner" so much as "late-night lounge host." She scanned the alley, then pulled the door closed and locked it with a short, efficient twist of her wrist.

Travis wasn't with her, but her appearance alone said enough; she wasn't unaware of what was happening behind her own walls.

"Delilah's out," Mitch said. "I'm going in."

"Wait...what?" Jayson's voice sharpened. "You don't have a warrant."

"I'm not touching anything. Just looking. I'll be fast."

He waited until she turned the corner at the far end of the street, then he crossed the alley quickly to the back entrance. With practiced efficiency, Mitch tested the lock. A small, recessed pin. Child's play.

Two clicks, and the door eased open.

The salon smelled like polish remover, lavender oil, and something else. Chemical. Acrid. Not nail supplies.

He moved inside quietly, through a small break room. Inside the salon, he stepped past manicure stations and pedicure chairs until he reached the front. Shelves lined the walls, packed with bottles, boxes, and bags. A wall to a smaller room had been removed, the bare studs and wires hanging loose, and the room itself stripped of anything except a stack of 2X4s and a box of screws.

He turned and scanned the rest of the salon until his gaze landed on a cardboard box marked with shipping codes. Easing the top back, he peered inside, and tucked beneath cotton balls and packets of gloves, were clear plastic bags filled with white powder. No branding. No paperwork. Just bricks of trouble.

"Bingo," Mitch whispered. "Get me a local badge. We've got product."

"Copy that. Sending word to Chief Fielding now," Jayson replied. "But you need to get out of there. I'll phone this in as a concerned citizen."

Mitch took a few discreet photos, then eased back out the rear door and locked it behind him.

He'd barely rounded the corner when a familiar beat-up sedan turned down the block. Noah's car. The same one from the courthouse camera. Mitch ducked behind a parked SUV as Noah pulled to a stop across the street, right outside Petal Pushers.

Noah didn't get out. He just sat there. Watching.

Mitch's pulse ticked up. The pieces were aligning fast.

"Jayson," he murmured, "Noah just showed up. Parked and watching again."

"Same pattern. Same time of day. Think he saw you?"

"Doesn't look like it."

"I'll run another plate check. Maybe pull his employment file again."

"Yeah," Mitch said, eyes narrowing on the man across the street. "And dig deeper. There's something off with him, like he's always just a step away from unraveling."

Mitch's fists clenched.

Between Travis's secret deals, Delilah's silent complicity, and Noah's strange behavior, this web was complicated.

He just had to make sure Izzy stayed out of it long enough for him to cut it down.

Mitch moved around the alley, silently and carefully, his eyes locked on Noah. The man hadn't moved. Just stared at the front of Petal Pushers, his expression unreadable. The guy gave off an eerie calm, the kind Mitch had learned not to trust.

A low wail cut through the quiet. Sirens.

Noah stiffened. A second later, he threw the car into gear, pulled away from the curb, and disappeared down the street.

"Jayson," Mitch muttered into his comm. "Noah just bolted. Probably heard the cruisers."

"Copy. I'll get someone to watch his place."

The sheriff's cruiser turned the corner and rolled to a stop in front of Delilah's salon. Mitch stepped out from the alley and approached, flashing his security credentials as Chief Fielding climbed out of his vehicle.

"Chief Fielding," Mitch said evenly.

Fielding gave a brief nod. "Hi, Mitch. We got a call about suspicious activity here. Did you see anything?"

"I was conducting surveillance in the alley..." He pointed toward the hotel, "I observed a pattern I think you'll want to look into." Mitch kept his voice calm, careful. "Travis Fielder has been entering this building late at night through the back door. No deliveries. No tools. Just slips in like he owns it. Multiple times over the past two weeks."

Fielding's eyes narrowed. "I haven't heard anything about Travis and Delilah being friends or friendly. Isn't Travis living with Sadie Anderson?"

Mitch nodded and took a deep breath. "One and the same. I'm concerned about the proximity Travis has to Izzy."

Chief Fielding nodded. "I'd be worried about that, too. I know you're watching that closely."

Mitch nodded. "I also saw Delilah Parker leave the building minutes ago, locking up like nothing was unusual. Given the context, her known debts, her recent sudden renovations, and her connection to Travis, it felt off."

"And you're saying this is all from surveillance?"

"That's right," Mitch said. "Camera footage. I installed cameras all around Petal Pushers so we could watch who might be coming and going. Izzy had reason to believe someone was entering the shop at night. She was right, we saw someone entering."

Fielding nodded slowly. "And you have that footage?"

"My team's forwarding it now. And there's more." Mitch pulled out his phone and scrolled to a still frame of Noah's car parked outside Petal Pushers. "This man, Noah Grady. Delivery driver. Fired last year, now freelances with his own truck. He's been hanging around the shop at odd hours, always watching. We've caught his car on courthouse surveillance multiple times."

Fielding studied the image. "You think he's tied into this?"

"I think he's got a fixation with Izzy," Mitch said. "He returned something this morning, a pair of her pruning shears, said he found them in her cooler. But she never put them there. Whoever placed them had to have been inside. This was at the same time he delivered an order she never placed."

"You're building a hell of a case," Fielding muttered. "You think this is a coordinated effort?"

Mitch shrugged. "Delilah and Travis have financial motive; if Izzy goes under, they could expand. That's all in the current town minutes. She's wanted expansion for a while. The only way to expand is if the businesses on either side of her sell. Izzy's place and the gas station on the other side. Or up. Adding a second floor. But she's financially strapped. Noah's motive might be personal. Either way, someone's trying to scare Izzy out."

Fielding tucked his notebook away and waved over

the newly arrived deputy. "We have a call into Delilah since the call came in about her place. I'm told she's on her way. You stay close to your client."

"After you see the footage Jayson, my partner, is sending over, I think you'll want to do a thorough check inside," Mitch said.

"Interesting. Thanks for the tip." Fielding nodded as he moved toward the street, where Delilah was pulling up in her car.

Mitch's gaze returned to the street where Noah had sat just minutes before. Too many players. Too many angles.

26

Izzy paced the length of Mitch's living room, her arms crossed tightly over her chest. The moon shone brightly tonight, casting long stripes across the hardwood floor, which made her feel all the more uneasy. Her nerves were stretched tightly, and she'd been displaced for nearly a week now. In limbo. She was at Mitch's and growing more attached to him every day, but this wasn't her home. She used to spend her non-working time with Sadie, or looking at floral magazines, or watching social media for pretty arrangements to make for her own shop. Now all she did was curl up under a blanket on Mitch's sofa or pace. And in both places, she worried. And, she'd lost some weight this past week. Her clothing was beginning to sag.

She couldn't stop thinking about Noah's face when he'd returned the pruning shears. The way he looked at her, too intense, too knowing, a weird grin, like he was waiting for her response. And that mysterious delivery. The invoice hadn't matched anything she'd ordered. She'd gone over her books twice already. And she never took her pruning shears into the cooler. There was no reason to. She and Ms. Jillie had shears at the design table. They routinely brought out the flowers they'd use for their arrangements and then returned the bulk flowers to the cooler. Stems and leaves were cut at the design table. To cut them in the cooler would leave nothing but stems in the cooler. It simply wasn't done.

A fresh wave of anxiety rolled through her. Was she losing her grip, or were people truly trying to unravel her?

Her phone buzzed, and she jumped.

Izzy's chest squeezed tight. She read the name on her phone and took a deep breath. She tapped to answer her friend's call. "Hey."

"Hey," Sadie replied, her voice quieter than usual. "You got a minute?"

"Always," Izzy said, sitting on the edge of the couch. "Are you okay?"

"I don't know." Sadie exhaled. "I think... I think you were right to be worried about Travis."

Izzy's heart skipped. "What happened?"

"I found something in our closet. Behind a box of winter coats. A small black duffel bag. I was looking for an extra blanket and knocked it loose."

Izzy sat forward, tension coiling in her spine. "What was inside?"

"A lot of cash, Izzy. Bundles. And Ziplock bags. Small ones. Like... what you'd expect to see on a cop show."

Izzy's breath caught. "Sadie..."

"I didn't touch it beyond that. I zipped it back up and put it right where I found it. But I took pictures."

Izzy closed her eyes. "That's good. That's smart." A knot formed in her throat and her heartbeat raced.

"I don't know what to do." Sadie's voice cracked. "I don't want to believe he's dealing. I don't want to believe any of this. But something's wrong. And I don't want to be caught up in any illegal bullshit. I haven't done anything wrong."

"I think Mitch and Jayson already suspected he was dealing or somehow delivering or whatever the terms are for it," Izzy said carefully. "They've been looking into Travis pretty closely."

"I figured." Sadie paused. "Is that why Mitch asked about Travis's employment history the other day?"

"Yeah. They've been connecting dots. It's all getting clearer now."

"Do you think I'm in danger?" Sadie's voice was so quiet, Izzy barely heard her.

Izzy stood and moved to the window, staring out at the quiet street. "I don't know. But Mitch will want those pictures. And you do need to be careful, Sadie. Really careful. Don't let Travis know you found anything. And if you feel like you're in danger, come here. Stay here. Mitch will understand. Neither of us wants you to get caught up in anything or hurt."

"I won't let him find out," she said quickly. "I didn't say a word. I just... I needed to tell someone."

"I'm here. Always."

There was a long silence. Then Sadie said, "Thanks. For still answering when I called."

"Always," Izzy whispered. "Don't forget, if you need a place to be safe, you can come here."

"I will," was her quiet response.

They hung up, but Izzy didn't move for a long time. Her heart pounded, but something had shifted. The fog of confusion was thinning. Pieces were falling into place.

And if Sadie could prove Travis was dealing, they might finally have the leverage they needed to stop all of this, for good. But she still didn't know why Travis would focus on her. Unless he was actually sleeping with Delilah, and also dealing drugs. Izzy wasn't stupid; she knew Delilah would love nothing more than for her to need to sell her business at a huge discount.

Izzy stood and took a deep cleansing breath. She squared her shoulders and decided she was finished feeling scared and sorry for herself. It was time she got active with her own security and stopped behaving like a frightened little girl.

The door opened, and she swung around as Mitch

stepped inside the condo. He was a sight. Those broad shoulders of his nearly made her swoon. But when he turned toward her after securing the locks, those deep brown eyes and his soft lips, that's where her eyes rested. And all she wanted to do was hug him close.

She stepped toward him, and he met her halfway. The instant his arms were around her body and she was pulled tightly to his, she closed her eyes and held him for a long time. She pulled back, their lips locked together, and their tongues danced a sensual dance. She tasted him, and he tasted like coffee, and he smelled like spice and the woods. Clean and fresh and so manly.

His lips kissed a path down the side of her neck to the crook where her shoulders began. He kissed back up to her ear, and his whisper so soft, yet so powerful, rocked her world. "I want you, Izzy Payton."

A shiver ran the length of her body. "I want you too, Mitch DeMario."

Without hesitation, he lifted her off her feet and walked them to the bedroom. Inside, he set her down and began pulling off his clothing, but his eyes never left hers. She began undressing, letting her clothing fall into a pile on the floor. She'd clean it up later. She was eager to make love to Mitch. She was excited to feel like this. It had been years since she'd felt like this about anyone, and he was like a drug she couldn't get enough of.

She'd barely stepped from her panties when his

arms wrapped around her once more, and their bodies, now naked and warm, were pressed tightly together. His skin was soft and without his clothes on, she could feel his muscles bunch and move under her touch. His hands dropped down and cupped her ass, lifting her off the floor once more, and she immediately wrapped her legs around him. He grunted slightly and she froze.

"Mitch, your ribs..."

"Fuck, Izzy. You're sexy." He growled between kisses.

She smiled as she allowed her hands to touch him everywhere. He laid her on the bed, his body hovered over hers, their eyes locked for a long time. "You've gotten into my blood, Izzy. I don't know when that happened."

She smiled at him, her heart felt full. She felt safe and protected and sexy. "Ditto Mitch."

He chuckled and rose slightly above her. She reached between them and curled her fingers around his cock, and pumped him a few times before seating him at her entrance. He smiled as he slowly entered her; the feeling was stunning. He filled her with his body. They were connected now. It was more than just sex. He'd sort of admitted it just now. As he moved in and out, she felt his love pouring into her. It was in his eyes. He never looked away. They spoke volumes to each other.

He moved slightly faster and she felt her body heat up. That tingling zinged through her, the precursor to her climax. It felt so good. Her cheeks heated as her hips met his thrust for thrust.

"You're the most beautiful woman I've ever met."

Her heart fluttered, her breathing was hard to control, and she didn't know what to say. That was a first for her. She swallowed to moisten her throat as she felt her body become ready to explode. Her emotions were so frazzled.

"Mitch."

He moved faster, his thrusts becoming more urgent. Their skin heated as they moved to bring each other pleasure. And just like an inferno rushing down a hallway, her orgasm raced through her body, and she cried out his name as she gripped him tightly. Two thrusts later, he joined her in pleasure with a groan. As he lowered himself to his elbows, his lips kissed her ear gently, and he whispered. "Izzy."

She closed her eyes, enjoying the feeling of it all. All of it. She wanted this feeling to last forever.

27

The morning light streamed in soft and golden, filtering through the blinds and casting lines across Izzy's bare shoulder as she lay curled beside him. Mitch watched her for a long moment, her breath even, her face finally relaxed. It was the first time in days she looked peaceful.

Last night had changed something. Not just between them, but inside him.

He slipped out of bed carefully, not wanting to wake her. Padding into the kitchen, he started the coffee pot and checked his phone. Two texts waited, one from Jayson and one from Chief Fielding.

Jayson: Sadie texted me some photos. You need to see these. They match known packaging from two prior cases in Lexington.

> Fielding: We've confirmed the powder from Delilah's matches a fentanyl-laced compound. High risk. High distribution value. We're getting a warrant for a full search.

Mitch exhaled slowly, dragging a hand through his hair.

Sadie had come through. That duffel bag in her closet wasn't just damning, it was dangerous. Combined with what he found in Delilah's salon and Noah's increasingly erratic behavior, this was shaping into something bigger than he'd first thought. A network. A local operation with multiple points of contact. Travis might be the low-level mover, but someone had to be supplying him.

And then there was Noah.

The man gave Mitch the creeps. The way he hovered near Petal Pushers, his fixation on Izzy, the delivery she hadn't ordered. Mitch couldn't shake the thought that Noah wasn't just watching her, he was studying her. Like she was his and didn't even know it yet.

He sent a text back to Jayson.

> Let's meet. I want to review everything again. Salon. Noah. Sadie's pics. We're close.

I'll come to your office in an hour. Bringing full files and surveillance pulls.

Izzy shuffled into the kitchen, wrapped in his t-shirt, her hair a sexy mess of curls and waves. She looked sleepy and beautiful and far too brave for the hell she was navigating.

"You okay?" she asked, rubbing her eyes.

He crossed the room and kissed her temple. "We're getting close. Fielding's acting on the salon. Jayson's bringing more evidence."

She nodded, trying to be strong, but he saw the flicker of worry in her eyes. "And Sadie?"

"She's smart. Careful. You were right to warn her. What she found might be enough to take Travis off the board. But that substance is also dangerous. She should get away from there for the time being."

Izzy leaned into him, resting her cheek against his chest. "I want this over, Mitch. I want to breathe again. I want to go back to my shop and feel safe there. And I want Sadie safe too."

"You will," he said fiercely. "I promise you. I'll do my best to make sure Sadie is safe, too."

His arms tightened around her. In his gut, he knew the final push was coming. But he also knew that promises weren't always enough. Not in his line of work.

After breakfast, he kissed her goodbye, made sure all the security systems were live, and headed out.

Today, they'd connect every thread. And if things went as he expected, one or both of the men circling Izzy would be facing justice soon.

But as Mitch pulled out of the driveway, a cold shadow settled over his thoughts.

Because he had a sinking feeling that one of them wasn't going down without a fight.

Mitch pulled into the small parking lot behind his office building, a modest brick structure tucked between the funeral home at the end of First Street. The sign on the door still read *DeMario Security Consulting*, though lately, his work had blurred the line between private sector and law enforcement. In towns like this, lines had a way of doing that.

Jayson was already inside, seated at the small round table with a laptop open and several folders spread across the surface. He glanced up when Mitch walked in.

"Morning," he said, tapping the spacebar to wake the screen. "You're going to want to see this."

Mitch dropped into the seat across from him. "Lay it out."

Jayson flipped the laptop toward him. The screen showed three photos side-by-side: one of the duffel Sadie had photographed, one from a past drug bust in Lexington, and one from a DEA file he'd pulled last night. "Packaging match is damn near identical. Same baggies, same colored zip tops, same white residue on the seams. This isn't small-time dealing. It's part of a known fentanyl ring operating out of Louisville and Lexington. My guess? Travis is a runner."

Mitch's jaw tightened. "And Delilah's salon is a drop point."

Jayson nodded. "Looks that way. She's got the location, cash problems, and motive. If she keeps the front legit, no one thinks twice about the back. And customers come and go in a business like that."

"And Noah?" Mitch asked.

Jayson pulled another file forward. "This is where it gets twisted. He was let go from his previous employer after a harassment complaint."

Mitch's stomach dropped. "Okay. What was the harassment?"

"The pattern fits. Female coworker. Claimed he followed her home. Left her gifts. Nothing technically illegal, but definitely creepy. He was warned, then fired. No charges filed. Since then, he's been delivering with his own truck as a third-party service and working under the radar."

"Which could explain the mysterious order. He could have ordered it for Petal Pushers since he'd be picking it up, he could deliver it, see Izzy, and act like he wasn't sure what was going on, he's just the delivery guy." Mitch rubbed his jaw. "He's escalating. He's always watching, always nearby. I think he's getting bold."

Jayson nodded. "I dug into ancient history on Noah. Harassment doesn't just start. It's a pattern. He's had similar issues at previous jobs. He becomes fixated on someone and can't let go."

"He's fixating on Izzy."

Jayson nodded. He tapped his computer a couple of times and pulled up an arrest record from Washington State. "About twenty years ago, he went so far as to kidnap a victim. He waited for her outside her workplace and surprised her from behind. Hand over her mouth, he easily picked her up and carried her to his delivery truck. He tied her to the rails and drove her out of town. Luckily, she'd managed to get her hands loose on the ride and slipped out of the ropes. She found a bat or a large stick in the back of the truck and waited near the door. When he opened the door and climbed in to get her, she hit him on the back of the head and ran like hell. He was arrested and spent only five months in jail due to overcrowding. He was a first timer, no previous record, so he was chosen for release."

"I'll be damned. So he is dangerous."

"And unstable," Jayson added. "Which makes him more dangerous."

Mitch leaned back in his chair. "Okay. We've got Sadie's photos, the drugs from Delilah's salon, surveillance of Travis entering multiple times, and now a potential pattern of stalking behavior from Noah. All roads are converging. Do we have anything tying Noah to Delilah and Travis?"

"We also don't know who's pulling the strings," Jayson said. "Someone's supplying that fentanyl. Could be local, could be someone in Louisville."

"Doesn't matter," Mitch said firmly. "We take the players off the board here first."

Jayson nodded. "So what's the move?"

Mitch stood and began pacing the small office. "We need to get Sadie out of that house. If Travis suspects she knows anything, she's a target."

"I'll reach out. Tell her we've got a safe house in town. You okay with her staying there?"

"Yes. Get her out quietly. Don't let her pack anything. Just tell her to bring her phone and come now."

Jayson made the call while Mitch grabbed a notepad and began sketching out their timeline. The salon had to be searched, Delilah questioned, Travis arrested, or at least brought in for questioning, and Noah. Noah needed to be watched until they had enough to put him away for good. Preferably before he got close to Izzy again.

When Jayson hung up, he gave a nod. "Sadie's on her way. She didn't argue. She actually seemed relieved."

"Good. We're going to need her statement, and she'll be safer out of that house."

"What about Izzy?"

Mitch's eyes narrowed. "I'm reinforcing security at the condo and staying close. If Noah tries anything, I want to be the one who sees it coming."

Jayson nodded. "And if he doesn't?"

Mitch's tone turned cold. "Then we find him before he gets the chance."

Mitch pulled up his phone and tapped Izzy's number.

"Hi."

He smiled despite his mood. "Hey. I'll come home and drive you to the shop this morning. Please don't leave the house without me there."

"Why, is something wrong?"

"I'll tell you when I get there. Don't open the door, don't leave the building. I'm leaving the office now."

zzy paced as she waited for Mitch. Something was happening today. She'd felt it when Mitch left this morning, a heavy dread in her stomach. After his call, that dread turned into a hot rock in her stomach. She wanted to call Sadie and make sure she was okay, but if Travis was there, she didn't want to make things worse for Sadie. She'd chided herself all morning for not demanding that Sadie come and stay with them last night.

The locks began turning in the door, and she held her breath for a moment before realizing, no one had the key but Mitch. Still, she stood frozen in place near the kitchen counter. The instant she saw Mitch step through the door, her breath rushed from her lungs. He turned and saw the concern on her face, and his lips turned down slightly as he neared.

"It's okay, Izzy. Things are finally coming to a head. This is simply a precaution for your safety."

"Sadie..."

"Is on her way to my office, where Jayson will take her to the safe house we have in town."

"You have a safe house?"

"Yes. It's loaded with security and just out of town a bit. It has a large garage on the property where I keep extra security vehicles."

Her brows bunched together, and she tilted her head to the right. "Why didn't you put me in the safe house?"

His brows rose into the lock of hair that fell over his forehead. His smile was genuine. Sexy. And a bit of a tell. "I wanted you closer."

"Is that so?"

She smiled as she stared at him. His cheeks tinted slightly pink, and she stepped closer to him, enjoying the aroma of his scent as it filled her.

He cleared his throat. "You're different."

"Oh. Different how?"

"Different."

"How?"

His lips brushed hers lightly. "Different."

He pressed his lips firmly to hers as his arms swept around her and pulled her close.

She enjoyed the feel of his tongue as he explored her mouth. She explored his in return. Warm, sensual, sexy.

When he pulled back, she stared into his eyes for a long moment. She smiled slowly before saying, "Mitch DeMario, did you have a bit of a crush on me?"

"Maybe."

She chuckled.

His hands slid down to her ass and pulled her tightly to his body. "I really have a crush on you now."

She giggled as her arms wrapped around his shoulders. She rested her cheek against his cheek as she closed her eyes and soaked up all the feelings happening in her body right now. Too many to name. So many new feelings she'd never felt before. It made her head spin.

He squeezed her once more, then stepped back. "It's Noah. He's dangerous and fixated on you."

Her eyes rounded. "Noah?"

"Yes. As we drive to the shop, I'll fill you in."

She swallowed to moisten her dry throat, as she woodenly reached for her purse lying on the table near the armchair. Slipping it over her head to rest on one shoulder, she turned to Mitch with a smile on her face. "Shall we?"

He moved toward her, his hand at the small of her back as they exited. After leaving the building, she couldn't help but turn her head from right to left, back to right again. She felt nervous, afraid, and highly exposed.

As he drove to Petal Pushers, he told her what his investigation had turned up.

The bell above the shop door jingled gently as Izzy stepped into Petal Pushers. The air inside still carried the familiar chill and faint scent of eucalyptus and roses, but something about it felt...off. She stood just inside the doorway, heart thudding, as Mitch followed behind her.

Everything appeared untouched, thanks to Ms. Jillie's help and Mitch's constant watch. But the sense of violation still lingered, like a shadow in the corners.

She swallowed hard. "It feels smaller somehow."

"It's not," Mitch said softly, standing behind her. "You've just been through a lot. It's normal for things to feel differently."

Izzy nodded and walked slowly toward the design table, running her fingers along the edge. She paused at the cooler, eyeing it warily, remembering the shears Noah had mysteriously returned. Her skin prickled.

Mitch came up beside her, his expression watchful. "You sure you want to be here today?"

"No." She looked up at him. "But I need to reclaim this place. It's mine, and I'm not giving it up to fear."

Pride flickered in Mitch's eyes. "That's my girl."

A smile tugged at her lips, and she leaned in to kiss him. It started slow, warm, and full of gratitude, but deepened quickly, her fingers curling into the front of his shirt as he pulled her closer. She hadn't realized how much she needed this. Him. Just one moment where nothing else existed.

A sound behind them made her freeze.

The bell on the front door jangled again.

Izzy turned just as Mitch shifted his stance in front of her, placing himself like a shield.

Noah Grady stood in the entryway, holding a clipboard and a single cardboard box. His face registered mild surprise, but his eyes, those eyes, were darker than usual. Sharp. Fixed on her.

"You're open early," he said, his tone neutral but thinly stretched. "I brought an order. Said it was urgent."

Izzy took a step around Mitch, keeping her voice steady. "I didn't place an order."

Noah's gaze slid from her to Mitch and back again, lingering just a little too long on where her fingers still touched Mitch's arm.

"It was added late," Noah said, smiling thinly. "Maybe your assistant?"

"No," she said. "She's off today."

Noah's expression didn't change, but the tension in his posture coiled tighter. "Well, I'm here now. Want me to just leave it on the counter?"

"Sure," Mitch said, voice cool. "Right there is fine."

Noah walked slowly across the room and placed the box down with deliberate care. He didn't speak. He didn't even look at the box. His eyes stayed locked on Izzy, like he was memorizing her. Marking her.

Izzy felt the unease crawl across her skin like static.

Mitch stepped forward. "Thanks, Noah. We'll take it from here."

Noah didn't move. "You two were cozy."

Izzy blinked. "Excuse me?"

"You know," he said, voice brittle. "Romantically, are you two together?"

Mitch's stance shifted. "That's not your business."

Something flickered across Noah's face, hurt? Anger? Possession? Then his mouth twitched into a forced smile. "Just asking. I saw you kissing."

He turned slowly, walking back toward the front door, but paused with his hand on the handle. "People don't always stay who they were, you know," he said without looking back. "Sometimes they change. Fast."

Then he left.

The bell jingled behind him, cheerful and wrong.

Izzy stood frozen in place, her pulse hammering. Her throat was parched.

Mitch turned to her. "That wasn't a delivery. That was a warning."

She nodded slowly, the edges of her vision fuzzing with anxiety. "He saw us. And he didn't like it."

"No," Mitch said, walking quickly to the counter and opening the box. Inside were two items, a note... and a long-stemmed red rose.

A chill swept down Izzy's spine.

Mitch's jaw clenched as he picked up the rose and turned it in his fingers. The small note was tucked into the petals.

It read: *"Will you have dinner with me? Call me..."*

Izzy backed away from the counter. "Mitch..."

"We're done here." His voice was low and tight. "Get your keys. We're going back to the condo. I'm calling Jayson, and Chief Fielding needs to know about this. It's time to stop playing defense."

Izzy nodded, her throat tight. But as she stepped toward the door, she glanced over her shoulder once more. Her shop, her sanctuary, felt less like home and more like a trap.

Noah wasn't just watching anymore.

He'd stepped into the game.

29

M itch shut the condo door behind them and locked it, then reset the alarm.

Izzy stood in the middle of the living room, arms wrapped around herself, pale and shaken. She hadn't said a word since they'd left the shop. And he didn't blame her. That box hadn't been a delivery; it had been a threat wrapped in thorns by way of a request for a date.

He turned toward her. "Please sit down, honey."

"I'm okay," she murmured, but her voice cracked.

"No, you're not." His tone was gentler now, low and urgent. "You don't have to be right now."

Izzy's shoulders fell, and she sank onto the edge of the couch. Her eyes met his, haunted and vulnerable. "He watched us, Mitch. He saw us kiss. That note…"

"I know." Mitch sat beside her, his thigh brushing hers. "He's not hiding it anymore. That rose was his way of marking territory, declaring himself as a suitor, so to speak."

Izzy's brow furrowed. "Like I'm property."

Mitch's jaw tightened. "Exactly."

He rose and grabbed his phone, pacing the length of the room as he called Jayson. "We've got a problem. Noah just showed up at the shop with another fake delivery. It was a rose and a note. He saw me and Izzy kissing, and he didn't like it. The note asked her to go out to dinner."

"Son of a bitch," Jayson muttered. "That's a clear escalation."

"Yes. By hand delivering it, he put himself in her shop, so she knows he can get inside her sanctuary. Plus, he asked if we were romantically together."

"So are you together?" Jayson's voice held humor, but it wasn't the right time.

"Jayson, it's..."

"I'm busting your balls, man. Settle."

Mitch let out a deep breath. "Okay. He's stepped up to the line. I want eyes on him starting now. I don't want him crossing the line."

"I'll see if Blossom Springs PD has a couple of unis available. Maybe we can get one to his residence. Discreet, but close."

"Thanks. And let Fielding know, I'll send him photos of the note and the rose. It's prelude behavior. The kind that leads to obsession turning violent."

"You got it."

Mitch ended the call and returned to the couch, sitting closer this time. Izzy had her hands folded in her lap, gripping tightly. "I should've seen this coming sooner," he said. "I knew he was watching, I knew he was off."

"You couldn't know this," she whispered. "But now we do. What do we do next?"

"We go on offense."

Mitch stood and moved to the table where he'd dropped the box and note. He examined the documents again, scanning for clues. Nothing stood out immediately, but it was clear Noah had crafted the moment for maximum impact.

He pulled out a notepad and jotted a list:

- Delilah's salon: Warrant in progress.
- Travis: Awaiting arrest.
- Noah: Escalating behavior, monitor full-time.
- Sadie: Safe house.
- Izzy: Relocate temporarily?

His pen hovered over the last item.

"I'm not leaving you," Izzy said quietly behind him, reading over his shoulder. "Don't ask me to go somewhere else."

"I wasn't going to ask." He turned to face her. "I was going to suggest we leave together. Temporarily. Just for a few days."

"Leave town?"

"Until we've got Noah in custody and Travis under pressure. Until this shitstorm dies down and I'm not waking up wondering if today's the day someone gets to you."

She was quiet for a moment. "Would that help or make us a bigger target?"

"It would force him to move faster," he admitted. "Desperate people make mistakes."

She rested a hand on his chest. "Then let's do it. If it's safer. But only if Sadie's okay."

"She is," he said. "Jayson checked in an hour ago. She's at the safe house. Locked down. We're the next priority."

His phone buzzed again. A text from Fielding.

Warrant is executed. Delilah's salon contained product, packaging, and burner phones. Travis picked up at home. Interview pending.

Mitch stared at the message, then looked up at Izzy. "Delilah's salon was dirty. Full takedown. Travis is in custody."

Izzy let out a long breath. "Then it's just Noah."

"And he won't get another chance," Mitch said.

He wrapped an arm around her shoulders, pulling her close, and felt her exhale shakily against his chest. His thoughts churned. This was almost over. But Noah had just made it personal, and Mitch wasn't about to let anything happen to the woman who'd already become so important to him.

If he didn't hear from Fielding or Jayson soon, saying they were watching Noah, he and Izzy would pack up for a bit and get out of town. The best-case scenario would be for Noah to make a mistake and get busted. Or, for Jayson to find out Noah's connection to Travis and Delilah. With the drugs found in Delilah's, to be able to tie Noah to them would be perfect.

He kissed the top of Izzy's head and softly said, "Pack a few things in case we have to leave quickly."

She chuckled slightly. "I only have a few things here. Remember?"

Yeah. She'd been in limbo for a while now. That always felt like shit. But she handled it well. Priority number one was getting Izzy home where she felt safe and wasn't under constant security. That thought made his heart hurt, though. He liked her here with him. He liked sleeping next to her, curled up into his side. He liked eating every meal with her. He liked the way she smelled and looked and felt. Thinking of this place without her in it felt terribly sad. He hoped she felt sad about it too. But first, her safety was everything; his feelings were last.

30

Izzy sat on the edge of the bed, staring at the small duffel bag she'd packed. A few tops, jeans, underthings, her phone charger, her meager toiletries, the journal she hadn't written in for two weeks, and a worn sweatshirt from college that somehow still comforted her. It felt strange to pack like this, not for a trip, not for a vacation, but to run - again.

Not that she was truly running. Mitch had made that clear. They were being strategic. She just hated how it felt.

She zipped the bag and stood, moving to the window. Mitch was in the other room on the phone again, probably with Jayson or Chief Fielding. She could hear the edge in his voice, the way his calm dropped into that deeper register whenever he felt things closing in. Not the sexy richness of his voice when he made love to her. That voice she loved.

Outside, the street was still. Peaceful even. But it didn't feel peaceful. It felt like the stillness before a storm. No birds chirped, no animals scurried around playing. Stillness as if even the wildlife knew there was trouble afoot. Wasn't it said they knew it before humans?

Her hand went to her stomach, not from nausea, but from nerves. She hadn't felt this unsettled since the morning after her parents' accident. That same dread was building again, only this time it wasn't grief, it was fear. And anger.

She wasn't just scared of Noah. She was furious. Furious that he'd made her shop feel unsafe. That he'd turned a place filled with light and laughter and eucalyptus into something she had to escape from. That he watched her like she owed him something.

And underneath that fury was something else, a cold certainty.

This wouldn't end until someone made it end.

The bedroom door creaked open behind her. She turned to see Mitch leaning against the frame, his eyes on her duffel bag.

"All set?"

She nodded. "As ready as I'll ever be. Any updates?"

He crossed the room. "Jayson's coordinating with Fielding now. A uniform is en route to stake out Noah's apartment. He's not there right now, though."

"Where is he?" she asked, the hairs on her arms rising.

Mitch shook his head. "No confirmed location. That's why we're getting out of here. If he's watching you, I want to make sure he sees nothing for a while."

"So he'll be the one chasing shadows," she said quietly.

"Exactly."

He held out his hand, and she took it. He tugged her gently to him and rested his forehead against hers.

"This is temporary, Iz. Just long enough to let Fielding and Jayson lock this down. We won't be gone long."

"I believe you," she whispered.

She didn't just believe him. She believed in him.

They started toward the door, and she halted. "Mitch." Her stomach tightened.

He stopped and turned to her. "It's strategic."

She shook her head. "Something just occurred to me. The birds aren't singing. There's no movement outside, like just before a major storm rolls in. The animals know. Listen, the birds aren't chattering outside."

Mitch shook his head. "Izzy, what in the hell does that have to do with us leaving?"

"They know something's up. You said you don't know where Noah is. What if he's out there, waiting for us to leave the security of the building? He'll have the jump on us."

Mitch stared into her eyes for a long time. She could see the moment he realized she could be on to something. He moved to the window and cracked it open, just a bit, and listened. The silence was deafening.

He cranked the window closed and pulled his phone from his pocket. He tapped a number and held the phone to his ear, the entire time his eyes barely left hers.

"Hey, Trey. Do you have someone who can come out to the Barracks and look around for Noah? Izzy has a terrible feeling, and I'm in sync with her on this one."

He waited a beat, then responded. "Thank you. We'll be here."

She took a deep breath. He believed her. At a minimum, he was willing to play this out and see if she was right. That was so much better than patting her on the head and telling her she had an active imagination. She let out the breath she'd been holding, not sure which way he'd take this.

Instead, he pulled her to his body for a long hug. He rested his head on the top of hers, and his strong arms wrapped her in his cocoon and made her feel safe and loved, and valuable. She wanted him to feel the same from her, so she wrapped her arms around his waist and spread her hands open to cover as much of him as she could. They stood that way for some time. Until her heart settled and she stopped shaking.

She pulled away slightly. "Thank you."

He kissed her lips and smiled at her. "Thank you. Thank you for being intuitive. Thank you for being you."

She swallowed the lump in her throat. "Mitch, I..."

His phone rang. She saw reluctance in his eyes; he wanted to hear her. She wanted him to hear her thoughts. Her feelings.

"DeMario...Hang on."

He tapped the phone so the speaker came on. "Go ahead, you're on speaker."

"This is Trey Fielding. We have people looking in the woods around the perimeter of the Barracks. Stay inside until I let you know it's safe."

Izzy looked into Mitch's eyes. He replied. "Will do. Let me know if you need me to help you search."

"Roger that."

The call ended, and Mitch glanced out the window once again, then motioned with his head toward the living room. "Let's hang out here. We can open the blinds and watch from the sofa."

Izzy curled into the corner of the sofa, her duffel bag beside her like a lifeline. Mitch stood by the window, hands on his hips, gaze flicking between the tree line and the street beyond. The blinds were half-open now, letting in the late afternoon sun, but every shadow outside looked suspicious. Every movement made her pulse skip.

Mitch hadn't spoken much since the call. He was locked in that internal mode she was beginning to recognize, where his body stilled and his mind spun with possibilities. She didn't interrupt. She was doing her own mental calculations, too.

Unable to wait any longer, she asked, "Do you think he's really out there?"

"I don't know," Mitch said, not looking away from the window. "But you were right. It's too still."

She nodded. Her fingers dug into the soft cushion. "It's not just paranoia?"

"No." His voice was flat. "It's instinct."

A minute passed. Then two.

The silence grew thick.

And then...

A sharp knock echoed from the back door.

Izzy jumped. Her breath caught in her throat as Mitch spun toward the kitchen, one hand already going to the small holster at his hip.

"That door leads to the private garage," he said quietly, moving silently toward it. "No one uses that entrance but me."

Her stomach dropped. "You don't think..."

A second knock. Slower this time. More deliberate.

Mitch held a finger to his lips and moved to the security panel. He pulled up the garage feed. Izzy came up behind him and peered over his shoulder.

The grainy footage showed a man standing just outside the garage's side door.

Noah.

He wasn't wearing his uniform. Just dark jeans and

a hoodie. His posture wasn't aggressive, just... patient. Like he knew he was being watched and didn't care. He knocked again, slower this time, as if they'd simply missed him the first two times.

Izzy's heart slammed against her ribs.

"He found us," she whispered.

Mitch didn't respond. His hand hovered near the security panel.

On the screen, Noah bent slightly and placed something on the stoop, something white.

A moment later, he turned and walked out of frame, toward the tree line.

"Do we follow him?" she asked.

"No," Mitch said tightly. "Not yet."

He tapped a number on his phone. "Fielding. We've got eyes on Noah. He just showed up at my garage door. Dropped something and walked off. Southbound on foot into the woods."

Izzy wrapped her arms around herself, staring at the frozen screen where the feed had paused. The white object, now clearly a single envelope, sat like a time bomb.

"We're dispatching now," Fielding said through the phone. "Don't touch the package. Stay inside. Officers will collect it."

"Copy." Mitch ended the call and turned to her. "That's it. We're leaving. Now."

She nodded, unable to speak.

Mitch pulled a second duffel from the closet and

grabbed his go bag from the entryway cabinet. "You take the front passenger seat. Stay low. I'll drive."

He reached for her hand as they stepped to the door, that fierce protectiveness in his grip steadying her nerves.

They didn't speak again until they were on the road, the condo behind them, the envelope left unopened. Whatever message Noah had left them, they weren't going to wait around to read it.

Izzy looked over at Mitch as the trees blurred past outside the window. His jaw was tight. His eyes forward.

"Where are we going?" she asked softly.

"A place Jayson and I set up a while back. Out near the state forest. Quiet. Secure. No one knows about it but us."

She reached across the console, found his hand, and gripped it tightly. "Okay."

Mitch didn't look at her, but he squeezed back. Then he tapped the button on his steering wheel, and the phone in the truck rang.

"Hey, where are you?"

" Izzy and I are out of the condo. Noah was too close for comfort. Let me know when Fielding finds him. We're headed to the shack."

"Okay. I'll boot up the additional security out there for you."

"Thanks."

The call ended, and in that silence between them, she knew two things: they were safe, for now.

And she was in love with Mitch DeMario. It hit her like a rock. These mixed-up feelings she had were feelings of love, and they felt mixed up because she didn't recognize them. She did now.

31

The crackle of gravel beneath his tires was the only sound Mitch let himself focus on as the truck turned onto the narrow, wooded path that led to the safe house. He and Jayson lovingly called it The Shack. Not another soul in sight. No tail-lights behind him. No tire impressions in the soft earth ahead. Good. That's what he needed. Seclusion.

He risked a glance at Izzy, curled slightly in her seat, her knees tucked up, hands in her lap, eyes glassy with exhaustion. She hadn't said much since they'd left. Her earlier realization, that eerie, intuitive sense that led to spotting Noah outside the condo, still weighed on him. It chilled him more than he wanted to admit. She had been right. Noah had gotten too close.

He tightened his grip on the wheel.

Izzy didn't deserve this. She didn't deserve to feel

hunted in her own hometown. To lose her business, her peace, her damn safety. Mitch hadn't protected her the way he swore he would. And now, they were holed up in a cabin like fugitives while a predator circled closer.

The tires bumped over a half-buried log, and Mitch eased the truck into the clearing. The structure was modest; an A-frame with reinforced windows, solar backup, satellite security, and a ground-level garage. Nothing fancy, but the place was tight. Safe.

He pulled into the garage and threw the truck in park, then turned to her. "We're here."

Izzy stirred slowly. "It's... quiet."

"That's the idea." He opened his door, stepped out, then walked around to hers and opened it before she could reach for the handle. She offered a small smile, exhausted, but grateful, and slid out.

Inside, the cabin was clean and stocked. They had it set up for cases such as this, and just this week, Jayson had come out here and set it up in case Mitch would need it, fresh linens, bottled water, enough food for a few days. He was right.

Mitch grabbed both his and Izzy's bags from the back of his truck. Inside, he switched the lights on and locked the door behind them.

"Let me give you the tour. It's small but cozy. This, obviously, is the living room." He pulled her along, happy to hold her hand and stay connected. They sauntered through the living room to the kitchen. It was open concept, easy to see the place from every angle. "Kitchen."

He pulled open the refrigerator. "Water and food are fresh. Jayson came out earlier this week, just in case we needed this place."

"Wow. You guys are prepared."

"We try to be."

He moved to a room off the kitchen. "This is the laundry room."

Then he led her to the first bedroom. "This is our room. The room just across the living room is the second bedroom. I'm going to check everything outside while you unpack. I won't be long."

He saw her swallow, but she nodded her head. He kissed her forehead and whispered. "It's okay. He didn't follow us, and no one knows about this place. Not even my friends in Blossom Springs. Just Jayson and I."

"Okay."

Mitch left the room and stepped out the front door, locking it behind him. He walked a full perimeter while Izzy unpacked, checking entry points, confirming camera feeds, and reviewing the motion sensors.

Then, finally, when he entered the Shack once again, he saw Izzy sitting on the sofa, staring at the cold fireplace. He sank onto the sofa beside her and rubbed the tension from his neck.

"I should've caught onto him sooner," he muttered. "I saw the signs."

"You saw a guy being weird," she replied, her voice softer now. "Not stalking me. Not breaking into my shop and leaving notes and roses. There are so many weird people out there, it's hard to select one from the crowd and say he's dangerous."

He let that sit between them.

"I keep going over every minute," he said. "Trying to figure out the moment it shifted. The first thing I missed. Maybe when we showed up to change the locks."

Izzy leaned into his side, her head resting on his shoulder. "He fooled a lot of people, Mitch. Me included. But we're here now. And we're okay."

He slid his arm around her and kissed the top of her head. Her warmth against him was grounding.

His phone buzzed on the coffee table.

> Jayson: Noah disappeared into the woods. Tracker dogs lost the trail near the old quarry road. Still looking.

Mitch exhaled slowly and typed back.

> We're at the shack. Tight perimeter. I'll check in every two hours.

He locked the phone and set it face down. For tonight, they'd focus on regrouping. Healing. Preparing for whatever came next.

Izzy looked up at him. "They didn't get him?"

"No," Mitch said. "But they're still looking, and

Jayson is watching cameras at the shop, and the police are watching Noah's place. We'll get him."

She nodded, then whispered, "I believe you."

He pulled her closer. "I think he's about to make a mistake. And when he does, we'll be ready."

Izzy didn't speak again, but her fingers slipped into his. And as the quiet surrounded them, this time the kind of quiet Mitch chose, he finally let himself believe they'd come out of this. Not unscathed, maybe, but together.

And that was all that mattered.

His heartbeat settled as he let that thought sink in. It was the most settled he'd felt in a long time. Not avoiding a relationship, not running from one, but running to one.

32

The first rays of morning light barely crept through the narrow windows, but Izzy had given up pretending to sleep hours ago.

She sat at the small kitchen table, cradling a mug of lukewarm coffee between her hands. It was her third cup. Maybe fourth. She'd stopped counting sometime after three in the morning when the silence inside the cabin grew louder than the wind, and her swirling thoughts of just how she had gotten into something like this. She was an average girl, woman, trying to earn a living with a small-town flower shop. Granted, she didn't have a mortgage to worry about; she'd inherited the shop from her father when he passed. And she lived upstairs, planning to one day earn enough money to buy a little farm outside of town where she could grow a lot of her flowers. The greenhouse worked for now, but she had big plans. Now, she was being hunted by a man with delusions, her greenhouse was damaged, and she'd need to pay for repairs. She lived like a nomad on the run, her clientele was scattered, and her life seemed too chaotic to ever put back together. And, Sadie. They were okay after a spat. But they hadn't gotten to the point where it was like it was before, and her life was a mess right now, too.

Mitch paced quietly in the living room, one hand rubbing the back of his neck, the other holding his phone to his ear. It was his third call to Jayson since midnight.

She hadn't meant to eavesdrop, but this cabin was small, and the stillness made everything sound closer.

"Any activity?" Mitch's voice was a low rasp.

A pause.

Izzy strained to hear Jayson's reply.

"Nothing on Noah," Mitch said, his jaw tightening. "Still off-grid."

Another pause, then Mitch gave a short nod. "Understood. Send me the file."

He hung up and turned toward her. Their eyes met, and she tried to offer a small smile. It didn't quite land.

"You should be resting," he said softly, moving to refill her cup.

"I tried," she replied. "My brain's not cooperating."

He poured the coffee and slid it across the table, then settled across from her. "Mine either."

They sat in silence for a beat before he spoke again.

"Jayson had something on Travis. Thought you'd want to know."

Her pulse ticked up. "Go on."

"They found texts between Travis and Delilah. More than just flirty crap. It looks like she was paying him for cash drops. Possibly using his night job as cover for it. And she's been threatening to go public with the affair and his illegal activity if he backs out."

Izzy's brows lifted. "So he's being blackmailed?"

Mitch nodded. "Which might explain why he stuck around even after things started heating up. Jayson's digging deeper into the payments. If they can trace anything back to the drugs found in Delilah's salon, Travis could be looking at serious time."

"But Delilah will be as well."

"Yes. They'll both be in jail."

Izzy exhaled slowly. "Sadie's going to be heartbroken."

"Yeah. But she deserves to know the truth."

They sat in silence again. The soft hum of wildlife had returned outside, a squirrel darted past the window, a bird chirped from the tree line, and a chipmunk chattered to its family.

"Think he's gone?" she asked, voice barely above a whisper.

Mitch shook his head. "I think he's regrouping. He made a move last night that didn't land. Now he'll adjust."

She wrapped her hands tighter around her mug. "Then we'll be ready."

He gave a small smile. "That's my girl."

She barely smiled, but his calling her "my girl" sent a shiver through her body. She looked into his eyes, "What was in the envelope Noah left?"

Mitch shook his head slightly. "I haven't heard from Trey yet. I imagine they have their protocols to follow before information can be exchanged. He's good though, and always lets me know when he can."

Despite the exhaustion, despite the weight in her chest, warmth bloomed at those words. She wasn't just being protected. She was part of this. Part of him.

Mitch's phone buzzed again, and he rose to check it. "Jayson's sending security footage from last night. Something about a figure near the shop after hours. He wants me to review it before looping in Fielding."

Izzy stood too, shaky but steady. "Then let's take a look. I might recognize something."

Mitch's eyes softened. "You sure?"

She nodded. "I didn't come all this way just to hide."

As they moved toward the laptop together, Izzy felt something else: resolve.

She might be exhausted. She might still be scared. But she wasn't powerless. And she was going to stop this asshole before he did anything else to her or her shop. Then she'd work on rebuilding everything. From the ground up, if she had to, but she'd do it.

The laptop screen flickered to life as Mitch loaded the footage Jayson had just sent. Izzy leaned in beside him, their shoulders touching, the scent of fresh coffee and tension filling the small cabin. The footage was grainy, a wide-angle from the alley behind Petal Pushers, timestamped just past midnight.

"There," Mitch pointed.

A figure moved at the edge of the frame, lanky, slow, deliberate. It sure looked like Noah.

He didn't rush. Didn't sneak. He walked like he owned the place.

Izzy's stomach turned as he stopped near the back door of the shop, crouched, and appeared to take something from his pocket. He slipped it into the slot of the utility box affixed to the brick wall, something small and pale, maybe another note, and then stood still for several seconds, just staring at the back door.

Izzy could almost feel his eyes on her, even through the screen. Like he thought she might open it. Like he was waiting.

"Creepy bastard," Mitch muttered.

They watched in silence as Noah stepped away, disappearing into the shadows again without looking back.

Mitch paused the video. "He's still circling. Testing boundaries."

Izzy folded her arms, gripping her elbows. "He doesn't act afraid. He's so bold, as if he knows where everything is and owns it."

"No, he doesn't act scared at all." Mitch agreed. "But he's slipping. This kind of behavior, leaving notes, watching from outside, it escalates. And it leaves a trail."

His phone buzzed again. This time it was Fielding.

Mitch answered, switching to speaker. "Go ahead, Trey."

"We processed the envelope," Fielding said without preamble. "It's handwritten, ballpoint pen, shaky lines, likely written in haste. No fingerprints. No postal service involvement. Just one sheet of paper."

Izzy's heart thumped harder.

"What did it say?" Mitch asked.

Fielding hesitated. "It's a love note. At least that's how it reads. He talks about watching Izzy, protecting her from the people who 'don't deserve her,' and how they'll be together, 'when the time is right.' Mentions her favorite flowers. A specific mug from the shop. Things only someone who's been watching closely would know."

Izzy sucked in a breath. Her throat tightened.

"It's delusional," Fielding continued. "But it's not overtly threatening. Not enough to charge him with anything direct yet. We're forwarding a copy to Jayson. You'll want to see it."

Mitch's jaw flexed. "Understood. Thanks, Trey."

Fielding's voice softened. "We'll get him, Mitch. Just need a little more. He's close to cracking. He always seems to be just a step ahead of us. We're calling in the Summerville police so we have more manpower."

Mitch nodded, and Izzy stared at his profile. His jaw was tight, and his shoulders raised slightly.

The line went dead.

Izzy stood still for a long moment, then turned to Mitch. "He knows about the mug. That's not on display. It's under the counter. I use it every day."

"He's been inside," Mitch said. "And not just the shop. He's been studying you. Obsessing."

The nausea rose again, hot and heavy, but Izzy pushed it down. "We need to find him before this escalates. If he thinks we're a couple, what happens if he decides you're in the way?"

Mitch stepped close, bracing her arms. "He won't touch you. I swear it."

"I know," she whispered. "But that note proves we're out of time. He's not just watching anymore. He's fantasizing. And if you weren't in the picture..."

"Don't finish that thought," Mitch said. "Because I am in the picture. And I'm not going anywhere."

Her hands shook, but not from fear. From adrenaline. Resolve. "Then let's catch him, Mitch. Let's end this."

Mitch nodded, his gaze burning with the same purpose she felt igniting inside her.

And for the first time since the sabotage started, Izzy wasn't just reacting.

She was ready to fight back.

33

The mid-morning sun filtered through the pines outside the shack, but Mitch felt no warmth from it. He sat hunched over his laptop, a notepad open beside him, the security footage from last night frozen on one frame: Noah, standing in the alley, staring at the back door like he was waiting for an invitation inside.

Izzy was in the shower to clear her head, but Mitch couldn't sit still. He'd already checked the perimeter twice. Reset the motion alerts. Made another pot of coffee he hadn't touched and rewatched the videos from the Petal Pusher's cameras several times. Something was nagging at the back of his brain, but he couldn't quite bring it to the forefront. Yet.

His phone buzzed beside the keyboard.

Jayson.

He snatched it up. "Go."

Jayson didn't waste time. "I dug into Noah's background like you asked. You're not going to believe this."

"Try me."

"Noah Grady is the grandson of Clarence Grady. Ring a bell?"

Mitch frowned. "Should it?"

"Clarence owned Petal Pushers back in the seventies and eighties. Before Izzy's dad bought it. The Gradys were kind of a fixture in town back then, but Clarence fell on hard times, lost the shop, lost the house, whole mess of debt. There was a lot of bitterness when Gerald Payton bought the building outright. Rumor was Clarence believed he'd been swindled, but nothing stuck legally. In reality, he had to take less than he wanted for the building because he had to get the bank off his back. And Gerald made the place thrive."

Mitch's stomach tightened. "So Noah grew up hearing how his grandfather felt like he got screwed over?"

"Exactly. Then the kid disappears for years, military stint that didn't last, and bounces around jobs. Records are thin after that. But here's the kicker, when he moved back to Summerville, guess where his first job application was?"

Mitch already knew. "Petal Pushers."

"Bingo. Gerald Payton turned him down. There isn't a ton of information about why, but some notes from some gossip columnist, remember those were all the rage back in the day? Anyway, in the local paper from about ten years ago, the columnist said Payton turned Noah down because he didn't know a thing about flowers or plants, and he gave off a weird vibe. But get this, he still hung around for a while. Offered to help with deliveries, kept showing up at community events where Petal Pushers was listed as a sponsor."

"Son of a bitch," Mitch muttered. "He's been fixated for a while."

"Yeah. This wasn't some recent obsession. It's been brewing for years. Maybe it started with the shop, but it twisted into something else. Something personal."

Mitch's jaw clenched. "My guess is it grew when Gerald Payton passed and Izzy came back to run the shop. Noah may have thought at that time he'd be able to step in and recoup money he believes his family is owed."

"I wondered that as well. How long has Izzy had the shop?"

Mitch took a deep breath. "About two years, I think she said."

Jayson whistled. "So Noah's been stalking her for two years? Hoping to get his hands on the shop? That doesn't seem likely."

Mitch nodded. "Maybe he saw Izzy and began to fixate on her instead of the shop. His focus changed. After all, he didn't have the money to buy the shop. So, what did he think he'd do?"

Jayson added, "And then Delilah entered the picture."

"Right. Maybe he became friendly with Delilah to help her get the shop from Izzy, thinking that would be just desserts. But instead, he ended up helping Delilah deliver drugs. Likely for payment."

Mitch nodded. The heaviness lifted from his shoulders, and things were beginning to clear up as to the whys. He always wanted to know the motive behind bad behavior so he could gauge just how determined a criminal was. "Good call. Anything else?"

"One thing. I pulled Noah's driver's license info. The address listed? It's fake. Doesn't exist."

"So he's flying under the radar."

"Yep. But unofficially? He's got a storage unit under an alias in Oak Hollow. I've already alerted Fielding. We're getting a warrant."

Mitch ran a hand down his face. "Nice work. Let me know as soon as you get inside that unit."

"You got it. Oh, and Mitch?"

"Yeah?"

"Be careful. Guys like Noah don't just snap. They spiral. Fast."

"Roger that."

Mitch ended the call and stared blankly at the laptop screen for a few seconds.

The obsession wasn't new. It was inherited. Twisted. And it had been building for years.

Izzy padded into the room moments later, hair still

damp from the shower, wrapped in a loose hoodie and leggings. She looked stronger than she had the night before, still tired, but steady.

"Everything okay?" she asked, crossing to him.

He stood, meeting her eyes. "I just talked to Jayson. He found something about Noah."

Her brows drew together. "What?"

Mitch explained, step by step. Clarence Grady. The old shop's ownership. The bitterness. The job application. The fake address.

Izzy didn't interrupt. But when he reached the end, her hands slowly pressed to the table behind her.

"He thought the shop should be his?" she asked, voice hollow. "He thought I took something from him?"

Mitch stepped closer. "Maybe at first. But it's more than that now. He sees *you* as the prize. Not the building."

Izzy didn't respond right away. Then her gaze met his, clear and hard. "Then let's make sure he understands just how wrong he is."

Mitch nodded. "We will. Jayson's working with Fielding on the storage unit now. If Noah's been operating out of there, we'll find something useful. And once we do…"

"We stop him," Izzy finished.

Mitch slid a hand over her back, grounding them both. "Exactly."

Outside, birds chirped again. Normalcy returned to

the woods. But inside the Shack, the hunt was on, and this time, they weren't just on defense.

They were ready to end this.

34

The wind rustled through the trees outside, but Izzy barely noticed it. She stood at the window, arms wrapped tightly around herself, staring at the patch of woods beyond the clearing. It should've felt peaceful here. Safe.

Instead, it felt like a pause. A breath held between moments.

Noah wasn't just a guy with a crush. He wasn't a random deliveryman. He was the grandson of a man who'd once owned her shop, a man who apparently died still bitter over losing it. The thought made her stomach twist.

He thought it was stolen. And now, Noah thought she was the thief. She remembered very little about her dad mentioning the former owner. There were a couple of times he came home upset from town meetings and mentioned Clarence as a troublemaker. But that was usually short-lived. He had a business to run, and there was always something to do. She worked in the greenhouse from the time she was little until she left for college. She fancied that she'd work in a big floral shop and be the head designer. All that taught her was that backstabbing worked for some, not for her. She refused to get ahead by stepping on someone else. When her father asked her to come home and run the shop, she'd been mulling it over when the car accident happened, and he and her mother were killed. Then it was either sell the shop or make it more prosperous than it had ever been, maybe add on products or enlarge the gift shop. She was on track for that, too, until all of this. Now her business took a dip, and she'd have to work extra hard to get back the customers that she'd lost during this time.

Mitch moved quietly around the kitchen, making fresh coffee, checking the security feeds again. Always vigilant. Always steady. She didn't know how he stayed so composed, especially with the pressure mounting the way it was.

She turned away from the window and sat at the table, running her finger along the edge of her mug. "So all this time... he was building some twisted story in his head. Turning my family into the villains."

Mitch nodded without turning. "Delusions like that don't need facts. They just need time to fester. And Noah had years."

She swallowed. "I keep thinking about all the times

I saw him around town. At the coffee shop. Farmers' market. I never thought anything of it."

"That's how he stayed close. Blended in. That's how obsession works, it builds slowly, then gets loud all at once."

She drew in a shaky breath. "And I became the loud part."

Before Mitch could answer, his phone buzzed again. He grabbed it from the counter, scanned the screen, then answered with a sharp, "Yeah?"

Izzy held her breath.

He listened for a moment, his jaw setting. "You're kidding. That's huge. Forward it now."

He hung up and looked at her, eyes sharp. "They're in the storage unit. Fielding found files, clippings about your dad. Old newspaper articles about the sale of Petal Pushers. And a corkboard full of photos. You. The shop. Your car. Even one of you and me at Mae's."

A chill skittered down her spine. "He's been watching me for months."

Mitch nodded. "Maybe longer. Jayson's going through the rest, but it's enough to prove a pattern. We're closer than ever now. We just need to locate him."

She stood slowly. "What if he comes here?"

"He won't," Mitch said quickly. "He doesn't know about this place."

But her doubt lingered. She knew how obsessed

people could always find what they wanted. "I don't want you to be caught off guard."

"I won't be." He crossed to her, cupped her face gently. "But just in case, I want you to carry this."

He reached into the top drawer and handed her a small canister of pepper spray. Her fingers closed around it shakily.

"I hate that I even need this," she whispered.

"I know." He kissed her forehead. "But it's temporary. We're almost there."

Izzy looked into his eyes and nodded. She believed him. Because if she didn't believe in Mitch, in the strength he'd given her to stand up instead of hide, then she'd fall apart.

She wasn't going to let Noah win.

A ping came from Mitch's laptop. Another message.

He turned back to it, frowning. "New lead. A hiker spotted someone near the quarry trail just after dawn. Matched Noah's build and jacket description."

Izzy stood taller. "Then he's close."

"Yes. Too close."

Mitch tapped out a quick reply, then turned back to her. "Jayson and Fielding are mobilizing teams. If they get a visual, they'll move in."

Izzy exhaled slowly. "And until then?"

"Until then," Mitch said, reaching for her hand, "we stay alert. And we stay ready."

Izzy squeezed his fingers, her jaw tightening. "If he

comes for me again... I want him to see he didn't break me."

Mitch's gaze was fierce. Proud. "He won't get the chance."

Outside, the woods whispered. But inside, Izzy Payton was done being afraid.

The morning air was crisp when Mitch stepped out onto the cabin's small porch, scanning the quiet woods. The humidity was already climbing for the day, but everything looked untouched. Secure. Just as he'd left it during the last sweep.

Inside, the scent of coffee filled the small kitchen. Izzy stood by the sink, re-dressed in jeans and a soft plum sweater, her damp curls pulled back. She looked calm on the surface, but Mitch knew that look in her eye, steely, stubborn, determined.

"I'm going in today," she said without preamble.

Mitch paused mid-step. "Izzy, we're close to catching this guy. It's not the time to make yourself visible."

Her chin lifted. "Exactly why I need to go in. I've been hiding long enough, Mitch. My customers are starting to lose faith, and so was I. But I'm done with that. The longer I stay away, the more power I give him. It's time I pull up my big girl panties and take this situation by storm. I've done nothing wrong. My father didn't either. He built a beautiful business, and I'm letting him down. I'm not doing that anymore."

Mitch crossed to her slowly, his hand resting on the back of a chair. "You're not giving him anything. You're being smart. Strategic."

"I'm being buried," she said quietly. "I need to show my face. Get back to my life. Or what's left of it."

He exhaled, watching her. This wasn't recklessness, it was resilience. And that made it harder to argue.

"I'll go with you," he said after a long pause. "Stay with you the entire time. I'll bring my laptop and work from the shop. No negotiations."

She gave a small nod. "Deal." The smile she bestowed on him made his heart jump. She was a beautiful woman. Not just outside. She had the spunk he admired and the business sense, too. Responsibility was strong in her, and he admired the hell out of that, too. She was the full package.

By late morning, they pulled up to Petal Pushers. The boarded window still stood as a reminder of the chaos, but the fresh flowers out front brought a softness that made Mitch glance at Izzy. She stood straighter just seeing it again.

"I'm going to call today to get the window repaired.

I have to make this place look like it's open, not falling apart."

He grinned as he watched her straight posture and the determination rolling off of her. "Okay."

Inside, she moved through the space like a woman reclaiming what was hers. Wiping counters. Flipping the sign to OPEN. Reorganizing the display in the front window.

Mitch set up on the side table with his laptop, keeping the shop's front door in his peripheral vision at all times. But he could also see the back door if he gave it a side eye. If he felt Noah was too close, he'd have Jayson join him for the day, right here.

Traffic was light for the first couple of hours. A few loyal customers came in, offering cautious smiles and carefully worded encouragement. Mitch scanned every face, every vehicle that passed the shop. They were genuinely concerned for Izzy and only offered their best. Plus, they left with flowers in their hands and smiles on their faces.

Then, just after lunch, the door jingled again.

Noah strode right in like he hadn't just spent the night running from police.

He wore a clean shirt with an old company logo again, *Clearway Supply,* but Mitch recognized the man immediately. Pale. Eyes too wide. A strange, eerie calm settled over him as he approached the counter with a medium-sized brown box.

Izzy froze beside the register. Mitch rose silently and moved to her side, between her and Noah.

"Got a delivery for Ms. Payton," Noah said, placing the box on the counter with exaggerated care. "Time-sensitive."

"No deliveries were scheduled," Mitch said evenly.

Noah's smile didn't reach his eyes. "Guess someone wanted it to be a surprise."

Izzy didn't speak. Her grip on the counter was white-knuckled. He could hear her breathing coming in spurts.

Mitch stepped forward. "You can leave it. We'll handle it."

But Noah's smile widened. "You might want to open it now. Wouldn't want it to go off at the wrong time."

Silence dropped like a bomb.

Mitch moved faster than he thought. He grabbed Noah's arm and shoved him back against the counter with one firm motion, his voice low and sharp. "What's in the box?"

"Easy, man," Noah said, too calmly. "Just a warning. Izzy and I need to talk. Alone. If she doesn't, well... accidents happen."

Izzy backed away as Mitch pulled his phone, one hand still gripping Noah. "Fielding," he snapped into the receiver. "I have Grady. He brought a suspicious package. Threatened the shop."

Noah didn't resist. He just smiled at Izzy, like they

were having a private moment. "You know it's always been you," he murmured. "I've been patient. But this time, you're coming with me."

Mitch shoved him into the corner. "You're done, Noah."

Outside, sirens wailed in the distance, faster than Mitch had hoped. Jayson must have already been nearby.

"Back room," Mitch said to Izzy. "Go now."

She moved, stunned but steady, and Mitch held Noah there until Fielding and two officers burst through the front door with guns drawn.

Within seconds, Noah was cuffed and being read his rights.

Mitch stepped over to Izzy, finding her in the back, one hand pressed to her chest, the other holding the pepper spray he'd given her.

She looked up at him. "You said he wouldn't get the chance."

"He didn't." He cupped her face gently. "You held your ground. We both did."

Chief Fielding eased over to where they stood. "I have to ask you two to leave the building. We have a bomb squad coming in from Tampa to take care of the package. We don't want anyone close by in case he has a timer on it."

"Does he have a remote?" Mitch asked.

"We checked his pockets; he didn't have anything except his phone. We're analyzing that right now for a timer or anything that could set off whatever he has inside that box."

Mitch looked into Izzy's eyes. "It's okay. We trust them. We have to."

Her eyes welled with tears, but they didn't fall. Then she took in a deep breath and held it for a moment before letting it out in a whoosh. "Okay. It's the first step to getting all of this behind us."

Inside Petal Pushers, Izzy Payton was standing tall in her own shop, even as the sirens removing Noah from the premises faded.

Mitch finally believed this might be the beginning of the end.

36

The Shack, as Mitch called it, was comfortable enough. A few flowers wouldn't hurt the place at all. She could likely help with that, but she hoped she wouldn't be here long. The furnishings were sparse but nice, the lighting soft but impersonal, and the silence left too much room for her thoughts.

Izzy sat cross-legged on the worn leather sofa, her palms cupped around a mug of peppermint tea she hadn't touched in so long that it was cool now. She couldn't shake the image of Noah's eyes, the way he'd looked at her when he brought in that box. So sure of himself. Like she was part of some shared delusion he'd been living in for years. Even the smile he had was off, like something you see in a horror movie before the killer sets off on his spree. The broken mental capacity of a person who had spent his entire life ruminating on hate and revenge.

She shivered, despite the warmth in the room.

Mitch entered quietly, a slight crease between his brows as he pulled the door shut behind him. He had that focused look again, calm on the surface, but his shoulders were tight, his hands in fists.

"Any news?" she asked, sitting up straighter.

He nodded once and crossed to her, settling on the arm of the sofa. "Fielding just finished his initial interrogation. Noah cracked faster than I expected. He said Noah almost seemed relieved."

Izzy's pulse quickened. "He confessed?"

"Yeah," Mitch said. "Enough to start building an airtight case. The box he brought in? Harmless. Just filled with wires and a kitchen timer. No real explosive components."

She sagged against the cushions. "So it was a bluff."

"Yeah. A dangerous one, but a bluff. Still enough to charge him with a threat of terrorism, stalking, criminal trespass, and about five other things."

Izzy stared down at her tea. "And Delilah?"

Mitch leaned forward, bracing his forearms on his knees. "This is where it gets deeper. Noah didn't want to take the full blame. He gave up details on Delilah in exchange for leniency. Said she offered him cash and favors to help him intimidate you. Deliver fake orders. Leave notes. She knew how fixated he was, and she used it."

"She manipulated him," Izzy whispered, her stomach twisting. "Just like she manipulates everyone."

"She did more than that," Mitch said. "He admitted he helped her move product, too. Said she promised to cut him in on profits if she expanded. But when he got sloppy, started stalking you instead of keeping deliveries quiet, she cut him off. That's when he decided to go rogue."

Izzy swallowed hard. "And now?"

"Now, Delilah's been arrested. Her salon's shut down and is still an active crime scene as they go through every bit and part of it to find all they can find. They pulled evidence from her computer and the office safe. Bank transfers, burner phones, even a few small bags of product she hadn't moved yet. But they're being thorough. She's going down."

Izzy set the tea on the side table and stood, pacing slowly. "So it's really over?"

"Almost," Mitch said, standing as well. "We have to wait for formal charges. There's going to be a lot of legal red tape. But Noah won't see daylight anytime soon, and Delilah's not far behind."

She stopped in front of the window and stared at the bright morning outside. "I don't know what I expected. Some big... moment. Confetti falling from the ceiling. A banner saying 'You Survived.' But instead, it just feels quiet."

"That's because your adrenaline's been running

full tilt for weeks," Mitch said gently. "Now that the danger's passed, your system's crashing."

She turned to face him. "I still feel like he's out there. That any second he's going to come through that door."

"He won't," Mitch said firmly. "Not again."

"What about Travis? Is Sadie safe?"

Mitch smiled, and she stared at his handsome face. "Travis has been arrested, and Sadie is safe. Jayson just went out to the safe house to let her know. She'd likely love to speak to you."

"I want to speak to her too."

Tears welled in her eyes. She blinked them back, but one escaped anyway. He came to stand beside her and pulled her into his arms.

"I've got you," he murmured into her hair. "And you've got this. I've never seen someone fight harder for what they love."

"I want to go back," she whispered. "Not today. But tomorrow. I want to go back to my shop and finish what I started. Rebuild everything they tried to tear down."

Her heart felt lighter just thinking about it. She could go back to her shop and let the town know she was still in business.

He leaned back just enough to look into her eyes. "We'll do it together."

Her lips curved in a small, trembling smile. Her

heart fluttered, and butterflies took flight in her belly. "You really want to help me?"

Mitch's eyes darkened with resolve. "Yes, I think it's a new beginning for Petal Pushers. Before you were catching up from the loss of your parents and keeping the shop going, and learning everything you needed to learn. Now you have a whole new beginning."

They stood together in the quiet, the weight of the past slowly falling away. Outside, the town would wake up to the news. The whispers would start, and stories would be told. But Izzy didn't care. For the first time in weeks, she felt free.

And she knew exactly where to go from here.

"Thank you, Mitch." She took in a deep breath. "Now the big question. When do I go home? And when I say that, it scares the shit out of me to think of being there all alone at night. But it's the only home I have."

He kissed her forehead and squeezed her tightly to him. She could feel the thud of his heart and hear the shakiness of his breathing.

"What if we looked for something together, just out of town, where you can have that big garden you want?"

Her eyes flew open, and she pulled back to look into his eyes. They stared back at her with steady reassurance. "Really?"

His lips curved up into the most gorgeous smile she'd seen from him. "Really. I've fallen in love with you, Izzy Payton. It took me a long time to find a woman who completely and utterly intrigues me, but I found you."

She stared at him for a moment, but no words would come to her. Her brain was utterly blank. What a stupid time to not be able to think.

His brows lifted into that lock of hair that fell over his forehead. She lifted her hand and smoothed it back, then slid her fingers into his hair to the back of his head.

"I've fallen in love with you, Mitch DeMario. I've been trying to figure out when, but it just happened. Even through all of this crap, you managed to take my breath away and made me fall in love with you."

He laughed. A full-on belly laugh, his head tilted back, and the joyful sounds that came from his body made her heart sing. "I could say the same thing about you."

He bent down and kissed her lips. There wasn't a better way to seal the deal.

Two weeks later...

Izzy grinned as the bells above the door jingled. She looked up from the clipboard in her hand, where her inventory list was nearly complete. The door opened again, and again.

Hanna, from Mae's Bakery, stepped inside holding a box with a smile as warm as her cinnamon rolls. "You didn't think we'd let you do this alone, did you?"

Izzy blinked. "Hanna, what's this?"

"Cinnamon rolls," Hanna said proudly. "And a fresh batch of cookies for later. Figured you could use snacks while you get things ready. Oh, and the coffee's coming. I strong-armed Quinn's son into hauling the carafe."

Behind her, the bell rang again. Then again.

Sadie stepped in with cautious eyes and a sheepish smile, holding a small potted plant with bright orange zinnias. "For color," she said softly, then stepped forward and pulled Izzy into a long hug. "I'm so sorry I didn't see what was happening sooner. I feel like I failed you."

Izzy squeezed her tightly. "You didn't. You're here now. That's what matters."

Sadie pulled back, eyes misty. "I want to help make this place shine again."

"You always had a way with display windows," Izzy said with a teary smile. "You're hired."

Behind them, more familiar faces filtered in.

Jayson brought two DeMario teammates, Blain Davis and Gabby Krill, whom she thought she'd heard Mitch call them, who immediately started hauling crates of supplies from a truck out front. Gabby grinned at her as she passed by, and Izzy felt like she stood with her mouth open at all the activity. Sid Hoffman, cool-headed as always, stepped inside with a tablet and a full folder of licensing forms. "Fast-tracking everything the city will need for your reopening," he said with a nod. "Consider it handled. Between

Grace and me, we've got this covered. That's why I married someone smarter than me."

Izzy laughed as she signed the forms Sid had for her. Grace gave her a hug after she'd signed the forms. "What a coup you pulled off here, Izzy. Your picture should be in the dictionary next to "making lemonade out of lemons".

Izzy chuckled. "I didn't do it, Delilah did it to herself."

Grace laughed. "She actually did."

Even Chief Fielding stopped by, setting a hand on the counter. "Noah, Travis, and Delilah won't be problems again," he said. "You've got the department's full support. We'll have patrols nearby for the next few weeks just to be safe. But they're locked up, and it's only a precaution in case they had anyone working with them we aren't familiar with."

Izzy could barely keep up with the warmth pouring in.

Mitch stood nearby, quietly overseeing everything with that steady presence she had come to lean on. She caught his eye, and the smile he gave her melted the last of the fear lodged in her chest. Sid and Grace chatted with Mitch, and she once again heard the bells above the door jingle. The smell of food took over the floral smell of her beautiful shop, and immediately Hanna and Grace began helping a gorgeous woman wearing the cutest outfit ever open a folding table and arrange the food. When the woman turned, she recognized Margo Marriott from Sarge's Sandbar. A minute later, her husband, Jace, entered carrying a huge stainless steel container of something that smelled fantastic.

Izzy took deep breaths as these townsfolk, friends of Mitch's and now hers, showered her with love and support. She'd never felt so much love. Sadie joined her as she thanked Margo.

"I don't know what to say, and please don't think I'm stupid, but this is all so... unexpected, and I don't know what to say."

Margo smiled, and she was stunning, her crisp blue eyes nearly danced in delight. "Thank you is plenty. Mitch is a good friend, and I hope you will be too. And we business folks have to stick together. He told Jace that today was clean-up day, and we started calling in the troops. And, you can't have people here working and not feed them, so that's where we come in."

Izzy's cheeks heated. She swallowed the knot in her throat, and her vision blurred. She blinked rapidly to dry the tears that threatened, but dang it if they didn't fall anyway. Sadie chuckled and handed her a tissue. "It's all good, Iz. We've got you."

By mid-morning, the front window had new seasonal arrangements, compliments of Sadie, and Quinn and his employees had replaced the temporary board with fresh glass, plus they fixed the damage in the greenhouse, too, something she worried would take weeks to do. The space was starting to feel whole again. No shadows, no fear. Just life.

And laughter.

Hanna was directing Ms. Jillie on where to stack coffee cups. Jayson was trying to convince Sadie to let him build a permanent security display case. And someone had brought a Bluetooth speaker, the soft hum of country music rolling through the air.

Izzy stepped outside for a break and was met with the sight of a small hand-painted sign leaning against the lamppost.

Petal Pushers – Reopening Celebration Tomorrow!
Beneath it, someone had added in smaller letters:
Free pastries, flowers, and hope.
Her throat tightened.

Mitch came up behind her and wrapped his arms around her waist. "I think the town's been waiting for this as much as you have."

"I didn't expect any of this," she whispered.

"That's the thing about good people," he said. "They show up when it matters most."

Izzy turned in his arms, heart full. "Tomorrow?"

"Tomorrow," he confirmed. "New blooms. New beginning."

And for the first time in forever, she didn't just feel like a florist rebuilding a damaged shop.

She felt like a woman reclaiming her life.

37

The morning of the grand reopening dawned clear and warm, the kind of summer day that hinted at growth and fresh starts. Mitch stood outside Petal Pushers just after sunrise, coffee in one hand, his phone in the other, watching the town come to life. He also had a new perspective on his newish hometown. He'd been here now about a year, but he hadn't spent much time getting to know the people outside of his friends and clients. He was changing that now. As people drove by, they waved, and it felt a bit like Mayberry, except for the sinister things they'd gone through recently. Every town had that seedy side, so ugly and dark it was kept hidden. But they'd overcome them, and he'd found Izzy. Life was funny like that.

The new window gleamed in the rising light. Colorful petals spilled over the planters out front, freshly replanted yesterday by Carly and Marcus, and the hand-painted *"Open"* sign fluttered slightly with the breeze. For the first time in weeks, nothing felt out of place. Nothing felt threatening.

He sipped the coffee and exhaled slowly.

Izzy had insisted on handling most of the final prep this morning, saying it grounded her. Truth was, she was reclaiming her space, her rhythm. He understood that. But he stayed close anyway. Just in case. She'd been staying at his place, and he was beginning to get itchy thinking about finding a place for them together. After today, they'd be able to focus on that. He chuckled to himself. He'd have bet anyone his life's earnings that he never would have been so eager to build a life with a woman so soon after meeting her. But there was just something about Izzy that made everything feel right.

Movement across the street caught his eye. Quinn and Hanna pulled to a stop across the street and began unloading their car trunk, which was packed with pastries and drink dispensers. He pushed himself off the post of the covered porch he'd been supporting and strode across Main Street to help them unload.

"Good morning. Let me help you with some of this."

Quinn chuckled. "You got it. I had a hard time getting Hanna to stop putting things in the car."

Hanna shook her head. "Organization is my job in

our relationship, and I don't believe I've forgotten anything. That's what all of this is."

Quinn chuckled as he handed Mitch a box of the best-smelling cinnamon rolls he'd ever had the privilege of consuming. Hanna's cinnamon rolls were popular not only in Blossom Springs but other towns as well.

"Damn, these smell like I imagine heaven smells."

Hanna laughed. "Thanks, Mitch. Did you hear Quinn's adding on to the bakery for me? We're expanding to selling online now."

"Wow. No kidding. Congratulations."

Quinn shrugged. "She's doing a fantastic business, but it's time to grow."

Mitch began carrying the large white box of cinnamon rolls across the street, Quinn following behind him.

Quinn lowered his voice and asked, "Is everything okay with Izzy?"

Mitch nodded. "Yes, she's still scared of things here and there. It's hard to get it out of your head that you aren't being watched anymore after knowing that for so long."

"Yeah. Hanna went through that too. I know she's told Izzy anytime she needs to talk, to let her know."

Mitch pulled open the door with the fingers he managed to angle out from under the box, "I'll encourage her to do that. Why don't we all get together some night for dinner and drinks? Relax, and you both can get to know Izzy a bit better."

Quinn held the door open with his foot as Mitch walked inside. "We'd love that."

As Mitch and Quinn set their boxes on the table, Sadie arrived, arms full of bags. And right behind her came Grace and Sid, grinning like cats who got the canary. Grace nudged Sid in the ribs with her elbow, and Sid put his arm around Grace's shoulders and kissed her. His friends were happy too. That made him happier still.

He looked up to see Izzy moving like sunlight, every step full of purpose, every word gentle but firm. She directed volunteers, double-checked price tags, and rearranged display tables that were already perfect. He couldn't stop watching her. Ms. Jillie was beaming as she arranged flowers as fast as someone could put them on a shelf. She laughed easily with those who stopped to chat, and she looked happier than he'd ever seen her. There was new life here at Petal Pushers, and everyone felt it.

The fear that once shadowed Izzy's eyes had faded. It was replaced with fire. And it was sexy on her.

He weaved around his employees, Gabby and Blaine, as they tested the security system Jayson had just finished upgrading. Jayson looked up from the back wall and nodded.

Mitch moved over to him to check on his progress.

"Everything's in place," Jayson said. "Motion

sensors, panic button, window alerts, if a squirrel farts too close to the shop, she'll know."

Mitch chuckled. "Appreciate it. Not sure she'll want to know that much, but it'll be reassuring that even the gassy squirrels won't get past her."

"Good." Jayson clapped him on the back. "Also, I might add, it's about time you found someone who makes you smile."

Mitch waited a beat, then added quietly, "I asked her to look at property just outside of town. A real home. With a garden where we can be together every day."

Jayson raised an eyebrow, impressed. "Damn. That serious? So soon?"

"It is. I am. When you know, you know. I used to hear that and think it was a bunch of crap. But it's true." Mitch took a deep breath. "For the first time in years, I want something more. I want peace. I want it with *her*."

"Then go help her run this show, man. You're not just her bodyguard anymore."

Mitch chuckled and made his way to Izzy. She turned as he approached, that same soft smile she reserved just for him lighting her face.

"How's it looking out there?" she asked, brushing her hands on her apron.

"Like a town ready to celebrate." He reached out and tucked a loose curl behind her ear. "And like the strongest woman I know is about to take her place right where she belongs."

Izzy's eyes shimmered. "I'm nervous."

"Good. That means you care. But I'll be right beside you the whole time." He leaned down and kissed her lips. "When are you going to announce it?"

Her eyes gleamed. "As soon as Sid and Grace tell me my permits are signed."

Mitch nodded toward Quinn and Hanna setting up tables across the room. "They're here."

Izzy turned to see Sid and Grace talking to their friends, and she took a deep breath. Mitch kissed her forehead and whispered. "It's all good, baby."

She hugged him close, then far too quickly pulled back as the door jingled and the first customers trickled in, friends, townspeople, familiar faces who'd weathered the storm with them. Izzy squared her shoulders, took a breath, and stepped forward with that bright voice she used to greet customers long before all this chaos began.

Mitch stayed close, watching her light up the room. Proud of her for all she'd overcome and thrilled she was in his life.

The past few weeks had taken everything out of them, fear, risk, and even some blood. But standing here now, surrounded by laughter, the scent of fresh blooms, and the woman he loved more than he ever thought possible, Mitch knew one thing for certain.

They had made it.

And whatever came next, they'd face it together.

He watched as Sid and Grace approached Izzy with an envelope in their hands. Izzy smiled at them, then turned to see him watching. Her smile grew, and it was like a magnet; he made his way to her to share in this news with her.

Sid whacked him on the shoulder. "Ready?"

"Yep. Is it done?"

"It's done."

He whacked Sid's shoulder in return, then smiled at Izzy. "Now's a good time."

He saw her throat constrict as she swallowed, then her smile grew. She nodded to him, and he held up a forefinger, "Hang on."

He pulled a step ladder from the back room and brought it out front. He opened it next to the old wooden counter Izzy insisted on keeping as a reminder of her father. "Stand up on the counter so everyone can see you."

He held his hand out to her as she climbed the ladder, then he whistled loudly after she nodded that she was ready.

The crowd turned to Izzy and quieted. She took a deep breath. "Thank you all for coming today to help me officially kick off Petal Pushers once again. I appreciate each and every one of you for coming and cheering me on." She swallowed and looked at him. He grinned and nodded. Izzy continued, "I'm here to tell you all first. I've gotten the permits to expand around the corner onto Main Street where the former Delilah's Nails used to be. I've purchased the building, it'll be demolished, and Petal Pushers will expand in that direction with more parking available."

The crowd clapped and cheered. Mitch clapped the loudest. He already knew what was happening, but to see Izzy shine while she told the townspeople what she was doing, after all the bullshit Delilah had put her through, that was icing on the cake. He couldn't have been more proud.

He helped her down from the counter and quickly pulled her into his arms for a kiss. Then he whispered in her ear, "I am so proud of you."

She chuckled. "Thank you so much, Mitch. I couldn't have done it without you, though. And I'm so happy to have found you."

"The pleasure has been all mine."

"Knock it off, you can do that later." Grace teased as she moved in and hugged Izzy. He was happy to stand back and watch Izzy gather all the support she could.

EPILOGUE

The sun dipped low over the hills just outside Blossom Springs, casting golden light across the wraparound porch of the little farmhouse Mitch and Izzy now called home. Wind whispered through the trees, rustling the leaves as the scent of lilacs and fresh-cut grass floated in the air.

Izzy rocked gently in the porch swing, a glass of sweet tea balanced on her knee, and her bare feet brushing against Mitch's shin. He sat beside her, legs stretched out, one arm casually draped along the back of the swing.

"I can't wait to see the wildflowers start to pop up. Thank you so much for spending so much time helping me plant them today."

He chuckled, and she nearly sighed because she enjoyed the sound so much. "I have to admit, I never thought I'd like being a flower farmer, but this life has really grown on me."

She laughed. "It has a way of doing that. Your hands in fresh dirt, seeing the seeds you lovingly planted poke through the dirt and bloom, and finally the beautiful flowers as they open up. It's such a wholesome life. It's hard work, but I can't believe I actually get to live like this."

She watched his chest expand as he took a deep breath. He looked into her eyes, his that deep brown she'd first noticed and fallen in love with. Fine lines were etched at the corners of his eyes, and a few shining silver strands of hair wove their way into his temples. He was incredibly handsome.

"I can't believe I get to live like this either. I'll be honest, though, the past few months of fixing fences, unpacking boxes, moving furniture, cleaning out the woodshed and the barn, I wasn't always loving life. But now that we've managed to set this place up the way we want it, I love the hell out of this place."

Izzy laughed. "I'm right there with you. When I moved into the upstairs of Petal Pushers, it wasn't anything like it was when I moved here. There were so many repairs on this place. My goodness, I had no idea."

Mitch nodded. "We could have hired someone to do most of that work, but there was something inside of me that wanted to do it myself. Now, every day when

I come up the driveway, I am proud as hell of what we've done here."

She leaned over and kissed his lips. "I am, too. That's why we did it. So we would be proud of our place. I can't wait to have our friends out here for a party."

"I'd love that. It's been a couple of months since we joined them at Sarge's for their Thursday night out. Why don't we go there tomorrow and enjoy?"

She giggled. "Yes. That sounds heavenly. Thank you."

"I think so, too. I'll let Jace know to expect two more tomorrow."

Izzy clapped her hands and leaned back against the arm he had around the back of the swing. They swung silently for some time, listening to the birds chirping. A gentle breeze blew the trees near the first garden they'd planted, and she watched the baby leaves dance.

Mitch took a deep breath and said, "I'll tell Jace we're celebrating and to have something special set up."

She watched a bird land on the fencepost he'd installed just yesterday, and her lips curved up. "Okay," she responded absently.

The swing moved as Mitch stood, and she turned her attention to him instead of the bird. He knelt in front of her, the handsomest smile on his face she'd ever seen, when he asked. "Don't you want to know what we're celebrating?"

"Celebrating?"

"Honey, I just said I'll tell Jace we're celebrating and to have something set up for that."

She shook her head, her brows pinched together. She recalled him saying something, but it hadn't sunk in what he meant. Not that they didn't have a lot to celebrate, they were living proof that life should be celebrated.

"I'm sorry. I guess I thought you meant this place, the repairs, and that Petal Pushers is doing a fantastic business. DeMario Security is, too. Sadie is doing well. There's a lot to celebrate."

He grinned. "I'm a bit selfish, I guess. I want one more thing to celebrate."

"You do?"

He laughed then, and the sight of his happy dancing eyes and the curve of his sexy lips had her enthralled with the sight of him. He was incredible. How did she get so lucky? Her parents must be looking down from heaven and grinning like mad.

Mitch pulled a ring from his front pocket and held it up to her. "I'd love to celebrate that you've agreed to be my wife. So, let me make it a formal question. Izzy, Isabelle Payton, will you do me the extreme honor of being my wife? Spend the rest of your life with me?"

Her eyes rounded. She felt foolish that she hadn't

caught on to his meaning. She should have been dreaming of this day after all they'd been through together. Didn't girls always dream about being proposed to? But they'd been so busy fixing up Petal Pushers, working with Quinn on the expansion, complete with offices for DeMario Security attached. Then buying this place, moving, fixing up so many things here from damaged wood floors to broken windows, to uneven cabinets, then planting the flower gardens so she could infuse every arrangement she made with her own flowers, she'd never dreamed of this.

Mitch's brows rose into his hair, and she blinked. "I'm speechless." A tear fell from her eye, and she took a deep breath. "Yes. Of course, I'll marry you. I...I...didn't expect this."

His brows furrowed. "You didn't think we'd marry one day?"

She chuckled. "I did. I mean, I guess I hoped, but we've been so damned busy, I didn't know when we'd even fit it in, and I didn't know if you were ready. Then I wasn't sure what your thoughts were on marriage, I mean, we've never talked about it. Then..."

"Shhh." He kissed her lips. "Say it again. Without all the other stuff."

She laughed. "Yes." She held his face between her hands. "Yes, Mitch DeMario, I'll marry you."

She kissed his lips, enjoying the feel of his tongue as it slid along hers. Their lips moved gently against each other's, the feelings of all he meant to her swirled in her mind, nearly making her dizzy.

He pulled back slightly and took her left hand in his and slipped the ring on her finger. It was beautiful. A white gold band with a single diamond flanked by two tiny sapphires.

"It's us," Mitch said, his voice a bit rougher than usual. "Strong, steady, and built from something hard-earned. I never thought I'd want more than peace, but then I met you, and peace turned into possibility. Into home."

Izzy blinked quickly. "Mitch..." She swallowed. "It's stunning."

"You're stunning, Iz. You're everything."

They kissed as the last bit of sun disappeared. There was no danger, no fear, only love, laughter, and the promise of forever.

And somewhere in the background, the quiet hum of their new life played on, steady, sweet, and perfectly theirs.

◌ LOVE. LAUGHTER. FOREVER. ◌

Mitch and Izzy have weathered danger, uncovered secrets, and found their happily-ever-after... but their journey doesn't end at "yes."

What happens when vows are made, promises are sealed, and the whole town comes together to celebrate?

Don't miss the exclusive wedding bonus epilogue!

Sign up for PJ Fiala's newsletter and get your invite to the most heartfelt celebration Blossom Springs has ever seen.

👉 Join now and grab your bonus epilogue!

KEEP THE ROMANCE ALIVE IN BLOSSOM SPRINGS!

If you loved the heart and heat in *Smoldering Nights*, don't miss the next swoony story set right here in Blossom Springs.

🎸 ***Don't Stop Believin'***

A *Rockstars of Blossom Springs* Short Romance

Global rockstar Sean West walked away from the only woman who ever mattered. Violet Slyk rebuilt her life—but when a surprise interview throws them back together, old sparks ignite fast... and so do old wounds.

Can love find a second chance under the spotlight?

This short, emotional read (about 14,000 words) is available exclusively on my website!

Perfect for an afternoon escape full of passion, tension, and second chances.

👉 Click here to get Don't Stop Believin' now!

ENJOY THIS BOOK? YOU CAN MAKE
A BIG DIFFERENCE

Your Review Matters!

As an independent author, I don't have the big budgets of major publishers for splashy ads or subway posters (not yet, anyway 😉). But what I do have is something far more valuable—amazing readers like you.

Your honest review is one of the most powerful ways to help my books reach other readers. If you enjoyed this story, taking just a few minutes to share your thoughts would mean the world to me. Reviews, even short ones, make a huge difference.

Click below to leave your review and help others discover *Smoldering Nights*:

https://geni.us/SmolderingEB

Thank you for your support—it means everything! 🩶

ALSO BY PJ FIALA

I'm fortunate to be able to do what I love. It's a blessing.

My list of written works has gotten so long I needed to move it to my website! How's that for blessed?

Anyway, click the link below to see the list of all of my books.

Thank you so much for reading.

https://www.pjfiala.com/bibliography-pj-fiala/

or scan the QR Code below.

MEET PJ

About the Author

Writing has always been my dream, but it wasn't until I found the courage to put pen to paper that my life changed in the most profound way. Creating stories that resonate with readers and bringing to life flawed yet lovable characters brings me endless joy—and I hope my books bring you the same.

When I'm not writing, you'll likely find me enjoying time with my family or hitting the open road with my husband, Gene. We're avid bikers who love exploring new destinations, meeting fascinating people, and soaking in the beauty of this incredible country.

Coming from a proud family of veterans—including my grandfather, father, brother, two sons, and daughter-in-law—I have a deep appreciation for service and the sacrifices that protect our freedoms. Their dedication inspires me every day, and I'm honored to share stories that celebrate resilience, love, and the American spirit.

My online home is https://www.pjfiala.com.
You can connect with me on Facebook at https://www.
facebook.com/PJFiala1,
and
Instagram at https://www.Instagram.com/PJFiala.
If you prefer to email, go ahead, I'll respond - pjfiala@
pjfiala.com.

Printed in the United States of America

First published 2025

Fiala, PJ

Smoldering Nights / PJ Fiala

p. cm.

1. Romance—Fiction. 2. Romance—Suspense. 3. Romance - Military

I. Title – Smoldering Nights

ISBN-13: 978-1-966513-10-0